Makenzie's Ring

TERI STEVENS

MAKENZIE'S RING
Copyright © 2025 by Chicken House Press and Teri Stevens

 First Printing: 2025
CHICKEN HOUSE PRESS

Library and Archives Canada Cataloguing in Publication
CIP data on file with the National Library and Archives

ISBN trade paperback edition: 978-1-990336-96-6

Summary: 13-year-old junior camp counsellor Makenzie Taylor uncovers a decades-old tragedy at Lake Tahoe's historic Baldwin Manor, teaching her about love, loss, and doing the right thing.

JUV069000 JUVENILE FICTION / Ghost Stories | JUV039060 JUVENILE FICTION / Social Themes / Friendship | JUV032170 JUVENILE FICTION / Sports & Recreation / Camping & Outdoor Activities

Author photo by Mitchell Glotzer

Chicken House Press
282906 Normanby/Bentinck Townline
Durham, Ontario, Canada, N0G 1R0

www.chickenhousepress.ca

To William, Alex,

Emerson & Mikayla

The real jewels.

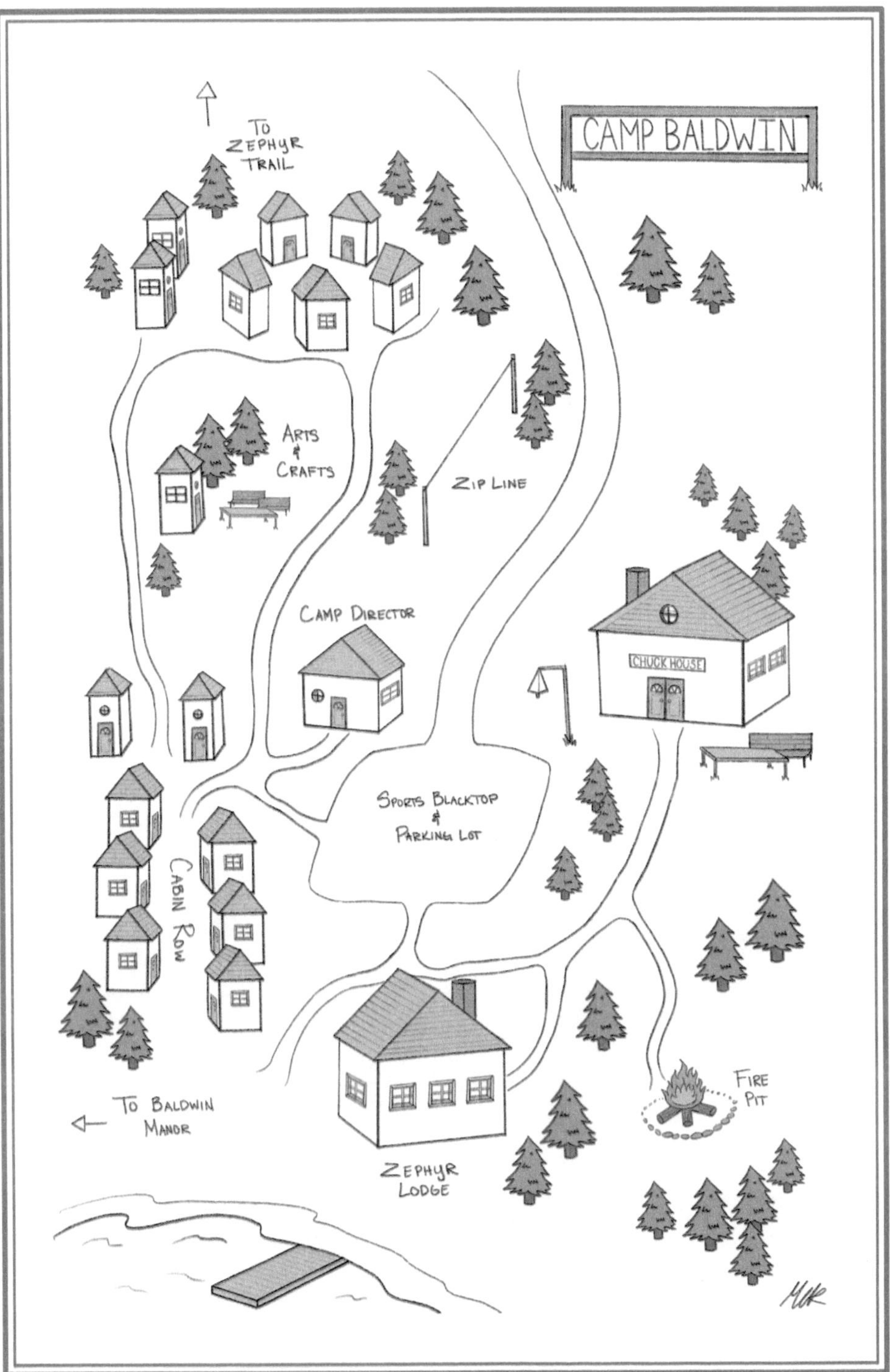

TO ZEPHYR TRAIL
CAMP BALDWIN
ARTS & CRAFTS
ZIP LINE
CAMP DIRECTOR
CHUCK HOUSE
SPORTS BLACKTOP & PARKING LOT
CABIN ROW
TO BALDWIN MANOR
ZEPHYR LODGE
FIRE PIT

MAKENZIE'S RING

TERI STEVENS

Prologue

The ring had been patient for decades. It had a story to tell, but there was no one to listen at the bottom of the lake.

One night, the summer sky cracked open. Rain pelted down in silver sheets, while lightning flashed across the black expanse. The whistling wind blew full gale. Waves crested, lifting the sand below the surface. Thrown from its resting spot, the ring careened along the lake floor, tossed from rock to rock. It ricocheted off a wooden boat dock piling and nestled in the sand.

The next morning was bright. Shadows came and went as kids swam nearby. The sun's rays pierced the clear water reflecting on the gold band, waiting to be found.

Chapter One

Makenzie couldn't believe she was almost there. She stared out the window while the rental car climbed the twisting highway, watching the bushy sagebrush and oversized rock terrain transform to lush green pine trees of varying heights. Her overprotective parents were actually letting her spend the summer away as a junior camp counsellor. The best birthday gift ever.

That morning, Makenzie's emotions flitted around like a butterfly not knowing where to land. At the Phoenix airport, her heart was heavy with disappointment because her best friend Jessica wasn't there. Until now, they'd always spent their summers together. But Jess had shattered her kneecap during the last basketball game of the season, ruining their plans of being junior counsellors together over the two-month break.

The girls had met in kindergarten, sitting next to each other on the first day because their last names began with a T: Makenzie Taylor and Jessica Tompkins. An only child, Jess was like the sister Makenzie didn't have. She promised Jess she'd keep in touch while she was at camp. And she meant it.

During the flight, her father started in on how he expected her to behave over the summer and not get into trouble. Totally frustrating. Her parents had turned up the dial on their overprotectiveness metre ever since her 13th birthday. Annoyed, and not wanting to argue that she'd never given him a reason to think that way, Makenzie had stuck her nose in a book until the plane landed in Reno.

Now that they were almost there, it was hard for her to sit still. Her nerves tingled with anticipation.

The car crested a gently curving hill, revealing the vivid blue outline of Lake Tahoe surrounded by evergreen trees. Wanting to share the moment, Makenzie glanced over at her father, but his eyes were focused on the road. Still irritated, she kept her excitement to herself.

In the distance, a large wooden sign with *Camp Baldwin* spelled out in thick white-washed sticks announced their arrival. Her father drove down the winding drive into the camp, located under the shade of towering pines. As the rental car rolled to a slow stop in the crowded parking lot, Makenzie took in a deep breath to calm her excited nerves.

The blacktop was a whirl of activity. Families unloaded duffle bags, backpacks, pillows, and sleeping bags from car trunks and SUVs, cluttering the surface with multi-coloured piles of fabric and canvas.

"We made it," Makenzie's dad said, turning off the ignition. "Let's unload your gear."

The tranquil silence inside the car evaporated when Makenzie opened the door. Shouts of recognition by counsellors reuniting with friends from previous years echoed through the trees. The warm, pine-scented air was a soothing balm after the car's air-conditioned chill.

At the edge of the parking lot, teens of varying ages crowded noisily in front of a dark green pop-up tent. *Check In* was printed across the top in white vinyl lettering. Makenzie watched the bustling scene while her dad piled her belongings behind the car. *If only Jess was here. We'd be unloading our stuff together.* Even though her dad was with her, Makenzie felt alone.

"Check in is over there," she said, pointing to the tent. "I'll be right back."

"I'll come with you. No one will bother your stuff."

Makenzie rolled her eyes. "Fine," she muttered. *Why can't he just let me go by myself?* She walked quickly ahead of her dad and joined the line.

A rustic cedar-planked structure loomed behind the tent with *Zephyr Lodge* spelled out in white-washed sticks above an oversized barn door. Wide wooden stairs, bowed by decades of footsteps, led down from a sturdy deck that wrapped around the building. Teens lounged on weathered Adirondack chairs and benches scattered around the platform.

It took a while to get to the front of the line, but Makenzie didn't mind. She was gleaning a lot by eavesdropping on the friendly banter that swirled around her. From the sounds of it, most had been counsellors here before. She wondered if there were any other newbies like her. Surely there had to be.

Under the tent, a middle-aged woman sat behind a table, deftly handling the crowd, checking in counsellors, assigning cabins, and fielding questions. The sleeves of her camo shirt were rolled up to her elbows, glasses perched halfway down her nose. A flat, silver-dollar-sized piece of wood hung around her neck by a thin leather cord with *Mrs. White* spelled out on it in faded black Sharpie.

Finally, it was Makenzie's turn.

"Hi there," Mrs. White said, looking up with a smile. "Name please?"

"Makenzie Taylor," her dad answered before she could open her mouth.

Ugh. It was like she was back in kindergarten. Makenzie gave Mrs. White a tight smile.

She watched the woman's finger scroll down the list of names printed on sheets of paper attached to the clipboard in front of her.

"Here you are. I see you're a junior counsellor, and it's your first time at Camp Baldwin," she said, placing a red check mark beside Makenzie's name. "Welcome." She tapped the end of the pen on the disk of wood around her neck. "I'm Mrs. White, the camp director."

"Nice to meet you," Makenzie said quickly before her dad could chime in again. "I'm really excited to be here."

"You must be Mr. Taylor," Mrs. White said, looking over Makenzie's shoulder at her father who hovered behind her.

"I am. My daughter has been looking forward to spending the summer here for months."

"Glad to hear it." Mrs. White's gaze moved back to Makenzie. "We partner first years with a buddy who's been a counsellor before to help learn the ins and outs of camp. You're paired with Hannah Bailey." Mrs. White craned her neck to look at a nearby bench where a group of teens were hanging out. "She was just here a minute ago… There she is. Hannah!" She raised her voice to get the girl's attention. "Come meet Makenzie."

A tall girl, appearing taller due to the bun that held her strawberry blonde hair captive on the top of her head, walked over.

"What's up?" Hannah said. Her faded forest green t-shirt spelled out *Camp Baldwin Counsellor* in white lettering.

"Meet Makenzie, your buddy for the summer."

"Hi. You're from Arizona, right? Mrs. White filled me in earlier." Hannah's friendly green eyes surveyed Makenzie's raven-coloured braids and sun-tanned skin.

"Yeah, Phoenix. It's great to be missing the heat this summer."

"Makenzie's cabin is Pinewood. Hannah, could you show her and her dad where it is? Here's your name tag." Mrs. White handed Makenzie a wooden necklace like the one she wore, only the wood was new and blank. "Add your name before the campers arrive later this week. Orientation is at five in Zephyr Lodge."

"Got it," Makenzie said. She took the necklace and stuffed it in the back pocket of her shorts.

"Let's grab your stuff. Where's your car?" Hannah asked.

"It's this way." Makenzie turned toward the parking lot, leaving her dad with Mrs. White.

"Who enforces the camp rules?" she overheard him ask as she walked away. *Unbelievable. Why does he have to know everything?*

"You packed enough for the summer and the winter," Hannah said, eyeing the mound of gear piled next to Makenzie's sleeping bag and pillow.

A rosy flush stained Makenzie's cheeks. "I wasn't sure what to bring. I'm not used to mountain weather, just desert heat all summer long."

"Don't worry, I did the same my first year. And I live here!" Hannah said, easing Makenzie's discomfort. "This is my second summer as a counsellor. I'm pretty sure I've got the packing thing down. Pinewood is close to the lake, we'll cut through those trees. Follow me."

Burdened by the weight of her belongings, the trek was slow, making it hard for Makenzie to take in the camp setting.

"Here we are," Hannah said, plopping the bulging duffle on the porch of a small, rustic wood cabin. *Pinewood,* etched in faded forest green letters over the cabin's front door, greeted Makenzie when she looked up after dropping her heavy load next to Hannah's.

"Makenzie," her father's voice rang out, startling her.

"Over here, Dad," she called, waving her hand above her head to get his attention.

"I was going to help you carry all that," he said, motioning to the pile on the porch, a hint of annoyance in his voice.

"We got it," Makenzie answered, equally annoyed.

"I'll let you two say your goodbyes. I'm in Silver Dollar, just a couple cabins up on the other side," Hannah said. "Find me after you get settled and we'll check out the camp before orientation. Safe travels," she said to Makenzie's father.

"Thanks." He nodded at Hannah. "Kenzie, let's move your stuff inside."

"I can do it. Shouldn't you get going to catch your flight?"

"I have time. I spoke with Mrs. White. It sounds like you're going to have a great summer."

"Yeah. I overheard you asking her about camp rules. Really, Dad? I'm 13, not a baby. I know all about rules."

"I just want to make sure you're safe. Be sure to follow them, okay?"

"Why wouldn't I?" Makenzie said with a sigh. "I got this, Dad. I'll call you and Mom tomorrow."

"All right, if that's what you want. And don't forget swim practice. We agreed on 30 minutes a day, right?"

"Right," Makenzie said through gritted teeth. "This is the hundredth time you've reminded me."

"You know your mom and I will miss you."

The warmth of her father's smile didn't melt her chilly demeanour. He wrapped his arms around his daughter and kissed the top of her head. Makenzie's return hug was mechanical and quick.

"Bye, Dad," she said, breaking away from his embrace.

"See you in August, kiddo."

Standing on the porch, Makenzie watched her father walk away. His tall figure weaved in and out of groups of teens and their families standing in front of cabins as he moved up a gently sloping hill and out of sight.

She was finally on her own.

Chapter Two

The tightness in Makenzie's shoulders dissolved as she watched her father disappear out of view. She took a deep breath in, then slowly let it out. The frustration she'd felt moments before escaped with her exhale.

Smiling, she opened the weathered door and stepped inside the tidy cabin. Three metal bunk beds outfitted with thin cot-like mattresses were lined up along the back wall. Large wooden shelves filled the wall on the right. Empty at the moment, the space would barely contain a week's worth of belongings for six campers. Tucked inside the doorway on the left was a small nightstand with three drawers and a twin bed. Her summer accommodations.

Makenzie grabbed her pillow and backpack and tossed them on the bed. Under her feet, a large, oval-shaped braided rug, faded from years of use, softened the concrete floor. The cabin's windows were open halfway. A faint breeze gently ruffled the blue gingham curtains, carrying in the scent of pine. The fresh mountain air mellowed the cabin's musty smell. Makenzie wrinkled her nose, detecting subtle hints of suntan lotion mingled with bug spray.

Grabbing the rest of her gear, she stowed it on one of the low, empty bunks. Campers wouldn't arrive until later in the week. These first few days were designated just for counsellors and staff to learn their various responsibilities and prepare the camp for the summer.

Makenzie rolled her down-filled sleeping bag out and lay on the bed, fluffing the pillow under her head. It smelled like home and reminded her of Jessica. A tinge of sadness tugged at her heart. *If only Jess was here, then it would be perfect.* But she was on her own now, and that was pretty close. Comforted by the pillow and soft bed, her eyes closed slowly. The day's early wake-up call and tension with her dad melted away as she drifted to sleep.

A sharp knock startled her. Makenzie's eyelids flew open to find Hannah's cheerful gaze peering in from the open doorway.

"Hey, sleepyhead, ready to check out the camp?" Hannah said, walking into the cabin.

"Yeah. Long day, I guess. Naps aren't usually my thing."

"No worries, but orientation starts soon. There's enough time for a quick tour if we get going."

Sitting up, Makenzie grabbed her swim team water bottle from the side pocket of her backpack and took a quick sip. "Ready? Let's go."

Outside, Hannah stopped and pointed at the nearby cabins. "We're in Cabin Row where the younger campers bunk."

Eight rustic wooden structures faced one another like dance partners, separated by a wide swath of packed dirt and scattered pine needles. Like Pinewood, each cabin's name was etched in faded green letters above its weathered door. Emerald, Tuscarora, Silver Dollar, and Baldwin lined one side, mirrored by Aurora, Richardson, Sugar Pine, and Pinewood on the other. The end of each row was punctuated by large bathhouses: one for girls, one for boys.

"Older campers stay on the hill," Hannah said, nodding her head toward a line of sturdy red brick bungalows. Their peaked wooden roofs overlooked Cabin Row. She paused, checking her watch.

"We've got time to check out the beach before orientation starts. It's this way," Hannah said, leading them away from Cabin Row toward a dirt path. An arrow shaped sign with *BEACH* spelled out in black lettering, guided their way.

"Lucky for you, you're in Pinewood. It's the closest cabin to the beach."

A strip of golden sand glistened in the distance. As they walked the short, tree-lined dirt path, the bright blue of Lake Tahoe came into view. Late afternoon sunlight danced across the water's surface creating a shimmering illusion.

Makenzie stopped where the dirt gave way to a gold flecked beach that hugged the water's edge to admire the view.

"It's beautiful," she said, stepping into the soft sand. "Photos on the camp website don't compare to being here in person."

"I know," Hannah agreed. "Afternoon beach time is always a camper favourite. And mine too," she said with a smile.

"That must be Baldwin Manor," Makenzie said, pointing to an impressive stone and wood structure in the distance, its rustic grandeur out of place after the minimal dwellings of Cabin Row.

"Yep. The camp's namesake. I'm super excited we get to help with its 100th Anniversary Celebration at the end of the summer."

Hannah gestured to a small dock that jutted out from a sandy patch of beach in front of the manor. "Here's a tip. See the boat dock over there?"

Makenzie looked toward the dock, and a small boathouse. Its wood siding exterior was decorated with life preserver rings, faded red and white so they appeared to be from a past era.

"What about it?"

"You can get really good cell service there. I discovered it last summer," Hannah said with a grin. "It's terrible at camp. I think it's all the trees."

"Good to know. My overprotective parents want me to check in with them a lot."

"Mine too. It's their job."

Makenzie's gaze travelled from the dock to the sprawling lawn that spilled out from wide wooden steps leading to the manor's twin glass-paned front doors. A dark flash behind the bright rectangles of glass caught her eye; like someone had passed quickly from the inside.

"So who lives at the manor now?" Makenzie asked Hannah.

"No one."

Goosebumps danced across Makenzie's bare arms, even though the air was warm. *Must be the shadow of a bird flying overhead that reflected on the glass.*

"The manor is open on weekends during the summer and volunteers wearing historic costumes give tours. But it's closed during the week, like now," Hannah explained.

In the distance, the clanging of metal echoed through the trees.

"Time to head back for orientation. Mrs. White's ringing the camp triangle. She's a stickler for rules, and one is to be on time. The triangle lets everyone know when something is about to start. It's old-fashioned, but it works. We can check out the rest of the camp after dinner."

"Sounds good," Makenzie said, looking back at the manor's gleaming front doors. *What has that house seen in its 100 years by the lake?* She turned to follow Hannah back to camp.

Chapter Three

Zephyr Lodge hummed with excitement, welcoming counsellors through its open barn door. Smiles beamed on the faces of returning counsellors when they recognized friends from past years, while first-timers like Makenzie wore nervous, jittery grins. A few rows of metal folding chairs faced a small raised stage where Mrs. White stood, greeting teens as they took their seats. Makenzie and Hannah had slipped in the door and sat in the back row just in time.

"Welcome to Camp Baldwin," Mrs. White announced over chatter that slowly quieted. "Together we'll instill lasting memories of camp fun in hundreds of kids. I'm especially excited about our participation in the Baldwin Manor's 100th Anniversary Celebration at the end of the summer. Built in the 1920s by a wealthy San

Francisco family to enjoy living amongst the outdoors, the manor continues to impress visitors a century later."

Flutters of excitement tickled Makenzie's stomach. She made it, camp was starting. She couldn't wait to tell Jess.

"We have some work to do before the camp is ready," Mrs. White continued. "Each of you has been assigned various projects to be completed before campers arrive later this week. When I call your name, come up and get your assignments. This is also a way of getting to know everyone if you are new to camp. Please pay attention so you can start placing names with faces."

Mrs. White turned to grab a basket containing folded sheets of paper that sat on the stage behind her. "Eric Wilson," she announced. A tall, lanky teen ambled to the front of the stage. He flashed the camp director a toothy smile as he took the paper. "Grace Campbell."

Makenzie concentrated on the names as they were called, doing her best to pair them with the faces they belonged to, but it soon became overwhelming. She was thankful for the round disk of wood each counsellor wore around their neck, emblazoned with their name.

"Makenzie Taylor."

She smiled at Mrs. White, taking the information, and returned to the seat next to Hannah. She unfolded the sheet, revealing the name Naomi Stewart at the top. Two projects were listed underneath:

1. Ready Zephyr Lodge Arts & Crafts/Game Nook

2. Clean Outdoor Rec Area & Stock Balls

"Jaden Xavier."

A muscular teen in a faded Camp Baldwin t-shirt with *Life Guard* imprinted on the back took the final sheet of paper.

"Okay everyone, quiet down."

The chitchat of counsellors comparing their assigned tasks slowly ceased.

"Above the list of projects is the name of a senior counsellor who'll lead your group through each task. We'll begin tomorrow morning after breakfast, which is served from 7:00 to 8:00 in the Chuck House. Lunch is noon to 1:00, and dinner is from 5:30 to 6:30. You'll know when meals are about to start when the triangle rings. These first couple of days are structured to get everyone used to the camp routine, so we'll be ready when campers arrive."

Makenzie glanced over at the page resting on Hannah's lap. "Jaden Xavier" was printed above the list of chores that differed from hers. Her heart sank. She wasn't in her group. Makenzie really wanted Hannah to like her and thought they'd get to know each other better if they were in the same group. She was her "camp buddy" after all.

A girl with purple streaks in her chestnut-coloured hair raised her hand. Mrs. White gave her a nod to speak.

"Are we still hiking the Zephyr Trail on Wednesdays?"

"Yes, Paige. Thanks for the reminder, it's a Camp Baldwin tradition. Another is s'mores on the first and last night of camp every week. I've printed a schedule for easy reference, until you have it memorized. Also, our daily activities will be posted on the chalkboard outside the Chuck House. Rather than recite camp rules and information, such as lights out and wake up times, you'll find everything listed on the back of the schedule. I expect you to review them before we meet up tomorrow morning."

As if on cue, the metal clanging of the triangle sounded in the distance. "And that's dinner. I'll be at the Chuck House after to answer any other questions. Schedules are on the table by the door; don't forget to grab one on your way out. Thanks everyone."

The sound of excited voices and metal chair legs scraping the antiquated wood floor filled the rustic lodge. Makenzie's nervous anticipation before the orientation was replaced by regret that she wouldn't be hanging out with Hannah over the next few days.

"What do you think so far?" Hannah said, turning to Makenzie while they stood in line waiting to pick up a schedule.

"All good, but I peeked at your project list. We're not in the same group."

"Oh, don't worry about that. Mrs. White likes to mix it up so everyone gets to know each other. Who's your group leader?" Hannah asked.

"Naomi Stewart."

"I remember her from last year. She's super nice," Hannah said, stepping to the front of the line. She grabbed two schedules and handed one to Makenzie.

"Good to know." Learning that Hannah liked Naomi, Makenzie's heart felt a little lighter.

They followed the trail of teens along a rock-lined path away from Zephyr Lodge toward a long, rectangular wood building at the edge of camp. Its slightly pitched corrugated tin roof stood out amongst the grove of pines that surrounded it on three sides. *Chuck House*, etched in the same faded forest green letters as the structures along Cabin Row, was spelled out above large doors, open wide to welcome the hungry crowd. Near the door, Makenzie glimpsed the large metal triangle that kept the camp on schedule, hanging from a thick wooden pole.

Makenzie breathed in the mouth-watering aroma of grilled burgers and felt an audible rumble of hunger in her belly. She realized it had been hours since she last ate. "I hope the food is good. I'm starved."

Chapter Four

Makenzie inhaled a deep breath and dove into the cold clear indigo water of Lake Tahoe. The sudden shock of its chilly depths sent a shiver up her spine. For a moment, her body felt numb, but the afternoon sun on her back warmed her as she began swimming. Each overhead stroke of her powerful swimmers' arms lessened the tingling. As promised, she was getting in 30 minutes of practice, one of the reasons her parents had allowed her to spend the summer at Camp Baldwin. Moving deftly through the water, she replayed the day's events in her head.

The counsellors had spent the morning completing their lists of tasks to prepare the camp. From clearing months of natural debris from the basketball half-court and ping-pong tables to sorting and organizing board games for easy camper access in the Zephyr

Lodge's cozy game nook. Hannah was right about Naomi. Her years of summers spent at camp and easy-going demeanour created a fun environment for Makenzie and her group, even though they were working. The swim was a welcome break, and hanging out with Hannah, who was lounging on the camp's boat dock in the sun, was a bonus.

Makenzie grasped the dock's metal ladder. Seconds out of the water, her wet skin broke out in goosebumps. She stepped off the top rung and quickly walked over the worn planks to join Hannah, leaving behind a trail of footprints. She lay on her stomach where the combination of sun-soaked wood on her belly and warm rays penetrating her back soothed the goosebumps away. She felt relaxed by the comforting warmth that surrounded her.

"Hey, mermaid. How's it going?" Hannah asked. She grabbed a tube of sunscreen from her beach bag and squeezed a quarter-size dollop of the creamy white lotion on her palm, replacing the scent of pine with the smell of coconut.

"Great, now that I'm warm. I love the cold water when I'm in it —so different from a pool—but getting out is going to take some getting used to. How'd your clean-up projects go?"

"Okay. I was in Jaden's group. You know, the lifeguard?"

"Yeah, I remember him from orientation," Makenzie said.

"We cleaned the beach and put the floaties in the water that designate the camp's swim area. Oh, and I helped repaint the faded lifeguard stand. I hope this wears off soon." Hannah pointed the back of her elbow in Makenzie's direction, revealing a cherry red streak.

"Clumsy," Makenzie joked as she looked down into the clear water below her. From her vantage point on the dock, she was enchanted by rays of sunlight that danced in and out of the shadows created by oversized rocks lying on the sandy lake floor. Peering into the shadows, her gaze fell on something shiny. It was out of place amongst the grey-hued rocks lodged in the sand. *It must be the sunlight playing tricks.* She looked away, then back again. It was still there. She was intrigued.

"Do you see that?"

"See what?" Hannah asked.

"There!" Makenzie pointed. "Shining in the rocks."

Makenzie was on her feet before Hannah could answer. She tugged her goggles on and dove into the lake. The enveloping chill jolted her warm skin. Her eyes opened behind the tinted plastic, scanning the rocks and sand. *There.* She was drawn to the twinkling light the sunbeams cast on the trinket through the clear water. Makenzie hovered over it for a moment, feeling a warmth wash over her, despite the cold mountain water. Her heart beat faster as she reached down toward the glimmer.

What is that?

Her fingers loosened the sand around the bright object. Once freed, she clenched her hand around it in a tight fist, planted her feet on the rocky lake floor, and pushed off, emerging seconds later at the water's surface.

"What was that about?" Hannah asked, jumping up to lend Makenzie a hand when she reached the top of the ladder.

"I found something!" Unfazed by a second round of goosebumps, this time mixed with excitement, Makenzie unfurled her fingers.

On her open palm lay a gold ring.

It wasn't just a simple, plain band. Set in the circle of gold was a heart-shaped, bluish-green jewel.

"Wow!" the girls exclaimed in unison.

The wet stone glistened in the sun. Curious, Makenzie tilted the band to look at the inside. The initials DB were engraved under the stone.

Makenzie was captivated. She couldn't believe her lucky find.

She slipped the ring on her finger. It fit perfectly.

"It's beautiful." Hannah said, studying the band. "I'm surprised you found it."

"It was so shiny in the dark rocks. I had to see what it was," Makenzie said, grinning, fingers splayed like a bride admiring an engagement ring.

"I wonder who lost it?" Hannah said. "Not to take away from your great find, but you're supposed to turn lost items in to the camp director." She sat on her towel and slid the wire-rimmed sunglasses perched on the top of her head down to shade her eyes. "Technically, you found it at Camp Baldwin, even though it was in the lake. Didn't you read the list of camp rules we got at orientation? It's number six if I remember correctly," Hannah stated matter of factly.

Makenzie's heart sank. She did remember something about lost and found when she'd reviewed the rules. It didn't seem to matter much at the time. What could she possibly find that she'd want to keep?

"You're right."

Her joyful smile deflated. She glanced down at her hand to admire the ring. It felt warm and tingly on her finger. *Must be the sun on the metal.*

"What a huge bummer." Makenzie's shoulders slumped. "I'll drop it off to Mrs. White on my way back to Pinewood. It'll be a cool story to tell my friend Jessica anyway."

"Totally cool," Hannah agreed, nodding her head.

Makenzie was quiet with the knowledge she couldn't keep the ring.

"Are you liking camp?" Hannah asked, breaking the silence. "It'll be more fun when the campers arrive and we're not just getting ready for them."

"I like it. Especially the food. I'm always hungry, even more so after swim practice." As if it had ears, Makenzie's stomach let out a loud gurgle, eliciting a pink glow under her tanned cheeks. "See what I mean?"

Hannah laughed. Makenzie wasn't sure if it was at her growling stomach or her rosy cheeks.

"Do you know who Alex Alvardo is?" Hannah asked, changing the subject.

"Is he a counsellor?" Makenzie hadn't met everyone yet and didn't remember anyone by that name.

"Yeah, but for the older campers. His cabin is on the hill above Cabin Row. I had a major crush on him last year. I thought it went away. But it hasn't. I was hoping he'd be in my clean-up group today, but he wasn't."

"At least you have the whole summer to admire him from afar," Makenzie replied, trying to look on the bright side, even though she wasn't feeling it.

Throughout their conversation, her eyes toggled from Hannah to the ring. It was so unique. She wondered what its story was. How had it ended up in the lake, and how long it had been there? Not wanting to prolong the inevitable, Makenzie uncrossed her tanned legs and stood. She grabbed her faded jean shorts and shimmied them on over her sun-dried one-piece.

"I'm going to turn the ring in and grab a shower before dinner. I'll meet you at the Chuck House." Makenzie wrapped her towel up into a ball and shoved it in her backpack along with her tube of sunscreen and goggles.

"See you," Hannah said with a wave.

Makenzie dropped her backpack on the porch at Pinewood and continued up Cabin Row toward Mrs. White's office. Her thoughts were scattered, like the pine needles that dusted the ground. Camp had just started. Surely the ring had been lost for a while, its owner unable to claim it now.

What difference does it make if I turn it in or not? No one will know.

Before she could ponder any farther, she was in front of Mrs. White's office. Its rock-lined path welcomed her to the wooden structure's barn-red front door. Makenzie slipped the band off her finger and admired the sea glass coloured stone one last time.

"Makenzie. Hi," Mrs. White said, walking toward her from the direction of the Zephyr Lodge. "Can I help you with something?"

Makenzie turned toward the director and smiled. Her fingers swallowed the ring and she slipped it deep in the front pocket of her shorts. "No. Everything's fine."

Chapter Five

"The Baldwin family resided along the shore of Lake Tahoe during the summer months from the time the Baldwin Manor was completed in 1920, through the 1960s when the buildings and land were transferred to the U.S. Forest Service," Mrs. White said, leading the small group of first-time counsellors on a tour of the historic property. "When friends of the family would visit, they'd stay in the quaint cottages sprinkled around the manor grounds."

Makenzie stood in front of the Baldwin Manor, marvelling at its grand, two-story stone and wood exterior. The stately home's gleaming glass-paned windows mirrored the pristine lake and the surrounding pines.

"Take some time to discover the property on your own. Let's

meet up again at the garden in 30," Mrs. White said, pointing to rows of bright flowers off in the distance.

Displayed around the property's many buildings, metal placards featuring sepia photographs and descriptions provided tidbits of information about the Baldwin family and construction of the manor.

Makenzie wandered through the grounds gleaning insights from the displays. She imagined what life was like back then for the wealthy and privileged family, evident from a row of small wooden cabins located behind the manor where the servants had resided. Each working member of the household had their own quarters, a compact room to themselves. Hand-painted signs affixed at each door labelled the inhabitant's position; maid, chauffeur, butler, nanny, seamstress, and cook. A narrow, shared servant's bathroom was tucked at the end.

Makenzie stopped to peek through the wire mesh screen door of the nanny's room, which was bigger than the other staff quarters. A weathered cardboard box advertising a croquet set leaned against a vintage children's desk. Its student, an over-sized teddy bear, sat in the chair, appearing to learn his ABCs from a chalkboard propped up by a stack of antiquated books on the desktop. A colourful wooden abacus was displayed nearby. Paint chips from years of use revealed the natural wood underneath orbs that hung from motionless strings. A fabric Raggedy Ann doll smiled from inside a vintage stroller. Makenzie imagined children dressed in old-fashioned clothing putting together the Erector Set pieces that spilled out of an open box.

The nanny's narrow twin bed, made up with tidy covers, and a small nightstand took up the opposite side of the room. An antique hook on the wall held a simple print dress, and a pair of worn Oxfords were placed neatly under the bed.

Makenzie was surprised at how much she enjoyed travelling back in time at each of the servant's doorways, their vintage displays providing a glimpse of life in a bygone era.

Absentmindedly, she reached into the front pocket of her shorts to make sure the ring was still there. She'd slipped it into her pocket before breakfast. A smile tugged at the corners of Makenzie's mouth as her fingers grazed the hard surface, but then she frowned. *It's not too late to turn it in.* She just didn't want to. Even though she knew it was the right thing to do.

Be sure to follow the rules, her dad's voice admonished, as if he was there, whispering in her ear. The sound of pine needles crunching on the path behind her scattered her thoughts.

"What do you think, Makenzie? Would you have liked living at the Baldwin Manor a century ago?" Mrs. White asked.

Cheeks reddening as if she'd been caught, Makenzie pulled her hand out of her pocket. "I'm n-n-not sure," she stuttered, crossing her arms in front of her. "It would have been fun in the summer, but not so much in the winter."

"Yes, well that's why the family stayed at the manor primarily during the summer months. We're ending the tour in the garden. Meet the group there in ten minutes, okay? If you see anyone from camp, please let them know." Mrs. White said.

"Sure thing." The thrum in Makenzie's heart subsided as Mrs. White walked way.

Alone in her cabin the night before, Makenzie had retrieved the ring from the front pocket of her backpack. Thoughts of returning it gnawed at her conscience. Her parents expected her to be honest and trustworthy. She held the circle of gold up to the single bulb that hung from Pinewood's wood-planked ceiling. The light reflecting through the heart-shaped stone made it morph from vivid teal to a pale turquoise hue.

The ring's shimmer captivated Makenzie, which surprised her, since she'd never wanted to wear jewelry before. It always seemed like a hassle to take off before swim practice and meets. It was just easier not to wear it. She did have a few nice pieces from her family which she wore on special occasions. But mostly, they lay untouched in the jewelry box on her dresser.

Somehow, this ring was different. She was drawn to it, but she didn't know why.

"Makenzie, you coming?" Grace asked.

Makenzie looked over at Grace who was standing in front of the butler's quarters. Also a first-time counsellor, she'd been in her camp clean-up group the day before.

"Coming." Her focus on the ring stopped as she jogged a few

steps to catch up with Grace. "This place is pretty awesome. Imagine having a butler waiting on you."

"And a cook," Grace said. "My mom would love that."

The girls followed a wide, rock-lined path that led to the garden. The path bordered a sprawling blanket of lawn spread out underneath tall pine trees, whose thick branches shaded the area from the afternoon sun. In a corner, water trickled down a triangle shaped fountain of rocks, flowing into a small fish pond where orange koi swam gracefully. A gravel path bordering the water's edge led away from the trees to a sunlit garden where a rainbow of flowers in bloom greeted passersby. A small starling flitted in and out of a wooden birdhouse that hung by a wire from the branch of a quaking aspen, its emerald leaves fluttering in the breeze.

The tranquility of the vintage garden was interrupted by noisy chatter coming from the growing group of counsellors as they filtered in from their tour of the manor.

"Grace, Jon, Makenzie. Looks like everyone's here," Mrs. White said. Her bespectacled eyes scanned the crowd, then double-checked her visual against the list of names on her always present clipboard. "During the 100th Anniversary Celebration, the lawn and garden will be the site of the Roaring 20s dance party. The dance is the summer event series grand finale celebrating the Baldwin Manor's centennial. Some of you will get to help with the festivities."

Makenzie glanced at the vacant lawn, imagining it full of party goers dressed in clothing from long ago. A figure approaching in the distance interrupted her daydreaming. She turned her attention back to Mrs. White, who was ending the tour.

"Feel free to explore the manor grounds on your own a while longer, but meet back at camp by dinner. You might not hear the Chuck House triangle here, so watch the time, pun intended." Her humorous attempt elicited an eye-roll from Grace.

"Thomas, good timing." Mrs. White smiled at the man Makenzie had noticed earlier as he approached the group. "This is Mr. Flint, Baldwin Manor's caretaker and historian. He oversees the manor's summer tours, along with the museum and gift shop, and lives on the property year-round."

"Hello," Thomas said with a quick nod. He wore faded khakis, paired with a worn, army-green, button-up work shirt. Thick white hair crowned the top of his head, and the edges of his brown eyes were creased from years spent outdoors. He reminded Makenzie of her grandfather back home. Only he looked worried, like he was preoccupied with something.

"There was a problem at the museum," he said with a frown. "Thanks for filling in for me on the tour today."

"Anytime. We've just finished," Mrs. White said.

"I'm always around if any of you have questions about the Baldwin Manor," Thomas said flatly, his expression unchanged.

Makenzie watched the interchange between Mrs. White and Thomas. For some reason, she felt sorry for him. She wasn't sure if it was his resemblance to her grandfather or the invisible air of loneliness that surrounded him.

"See you later," Thomas said. He turned and walked quickly down the path leading out of the garden. Makenzie's gaze followed him. *I'm going to find a way to make him smile before the end of camp.*

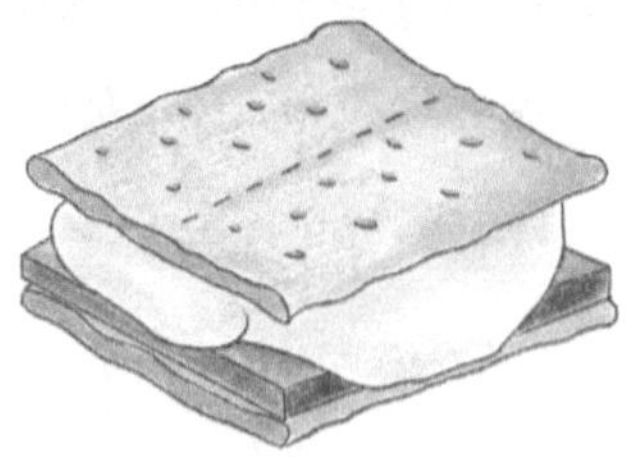

Chapter Six

Flickers of fire danced around the charred pieces of wood that lay in the large metal ring. Their embers glowed a bright orange-red, sending faint tendrils of smoke skyward from the hot coals; the perfect temperature for making s'mores.

Makenzie and Hannah were perched on a log in front of the fire ring, roasting marshmallows. The dimming firelight cast an eerie glow on the counsellors who sat on the opposite side, eating sticky s'mores. As Mrs. White had intended, camaraderie flowed easily through the group who'd gotten to know each other while preparing the camp for the arrival of campers the following day. The campfire and treats were well earned by the counsellors' hard work.

An older counsellor had just grossed them out with the classic tale of the terrified man who caught his attacker's hand in a car window as it was being rolled up. When the panicked driver sped away, the bloody, writhing appendage fell in his lap.

Once the group's reaction of "eww" and "gross!" quieted, Eric asked, "Have you heard about the Baldwin Manor ghost?"

"No, tell us," Makenzie said, licking a mixture of melted chocolate and marshmallow off her finger. The gooey combination was delicious.

"Over the years, counsellors say they've seen a girl at the Camp Baldwin beach at night. When they walk toward her, she disappears."

The ring, hidden in the front pocket of Makenzie's cotton shorts, felt warm. Caught off guard, she wriggled her hand in the soft fabric. *How odd, it was warm, almost hot. Must be from the heat of the fire.* She pushed the circle of metal farther down in the folds of her pocket.

"My older sister told me that creepy camp legend," Hannah said. "She was a counsellor here before she went to college. She never saw a ghost. I didn't see it last summer. It's just a made-up story to scare campers."

"I don't believe in ghosts," Makenzie said, popping the last bite of s'more in her mouth.

"Well, the story has been around for years," Eric said, giving her a wicked grin from across the dying fire. "Stranger things have happened."

Suddenly, from the darkness behind the fire ring, they heard the crunch of dry pine needles, startling them all. Unnerved, the s'more in Makenzie's belly did a somersault.

"It got awfully quiet," Mrs. White said, emerging from the trees. The beam of her down-turned flashlight illuminated a swirl of dust particles around her hiking boots. "Did I interrupt something?"

"Just some silly ghost stories," Hannah answered.

"It's time for lights out soon. Eric, you're on fire duty. Make sure it's extinguished before you turn in. Don't be long, kids. I want everyone to be rested for the first day of camp tomorrow. See you in the morning." Mrs. White turned and followed the glow of her flashlight toward camp.

The counsellors lazed around the fire ring until yawns and the night chill invaded the group. A whoosh from the bucket of sand Eric poured on the glowing embers signalled lights out. Beams of light flickered through the trees, away from the smouldering coals, as the teens retreated to their cabins.

Makenzie and Hannah strolled slowly to Cabin Row, their flashlights illuminating the path littered with pine needles.

"I forgot to ask. How'd it go with Mrs. White?" Hannah said.

In a s'more-induced fog, Makenzie had no idea what Hannah was talking about. "Hmm, I'm not sure what you mean."

"The other day, when you turned in the ring you found?"

Makenzie's heart quickened. "Oh t-t-that," she stammered, thankful it was dark and Hannah couldn't see her face.

"It's not every day someone finds a ring like that."

"Um…" Makenzie said, scrambling. "She thought it was beautiful, and thanked me for turning it in. That was all."

"I know it wasn't easy, but you did the right thing," Hannah said with an air of authority.

"Thanks," Makenzie answered quietly, her throat thick with the lie she had just swallowed.

Moths danced in and out of the light fixture that illuminated the weathered door of Pinewood.

"See you tomorrow," Hannah said, continuing up Cabin Row to Silver Dollar.

"Goodnight," Makenzie said.

She stood on Pinewood's small porch watching Hannah until she disappeared into her cabin while s'mores churned in her stomach.

Makenzie flicked the light switch on and leaned against the cabin door, her full weight pressed against the worn wood. She took in a deep breath and held it, hoping to calm her swirling stomach. She exhaled slowly, repeating the breathing exercise her swim coach had taught the team to settle their nerves before meets. The technique worked. She slid her hand in the pocket of her shorts and retrieved the ring. The stone looked different. Makenzie held it up to the glowing bulb in the centre of the ceiling. It was darker. A deep sapphire, like the depths of the lake, replaced its previous pale turquoise hue. *That's kinda weird.*

The quiet of the cabin exaggerated the protesting squeak of the twin bed's antiquated box-spring coils as Makenzie sat on the edge and kicked off her dusty tennis shoes. She rested her head in the soft fluff of the pillow, grateful when the tension in her body melted away after a few moments.

She slipped on the ring and raised her hand above her tired eyes to examine it again. The lie to Hannah and its gnawing guilt was replaced by her unexplainable compulsion to keep the ring, even though she knew her parents would be appalled at her behaviour. *I'm sure Hannah will forget about it as the summer wears on. The arrival of campers tomorrow will help.*

Makenzie yawned while her eyelids fluttered shut and she drifted to sleep.

A young woman stands in front of the Baldwin Manor looking out at the lake. The fabric of her long navy skirt swirls above black mid-ankle boots as she walks toward the manor's boat dock. White ruffles on the front of her billowy long-sleeved blouse lift in the soft evening breeze. Fabric-covered buttons march down the middle of her back like candied dots, disappearing into the waistband of her skirt. Her long chestnut-brown hair is gathered in a loose ponytail at the nape of her neck, held in place by a large navy and white pinstriped fabric bow.

Tendrils of hair frame her oval face.

The girl approaches the dock, arms reaching down her sides to grasp handfuls of fabric. She lifts the skirt to better navigate wooden steps that lead up to the dock. The water beneath it is painted a cobalt blue by the fading sunlight. She crosses her arms impatiently, checks her wristwatch, then paces up and down the length of the dock, her skirt fanning out like an inverted tulip with each turn of her booted heel.

A smile alights on the girl's sullen face when a seated figure in a paddle boat floats into view. The pacing stops and her right hand flies in the air with a wave, the soft fabric of her sleeve a welcoming flag. As the boat nears, the girl bends down and unwinds a rope wrapped around a metal cleat, its end knotted in the cast iron hardware bolted to the edge of the dock. She coils the rope in her hands and waits.

The figure in the boat paddles toward the dock. Oars churn through the water, powered by the arms of a young man. A flat fabric cap with a brim shades his eyes. As the boat draws closer, the girl tosses the rope. Its coils unfurl in mid-air and land in the water with a soft splash.

The rower lays the oars on the boat floor, grabs the line, and pulls the vessel closer to the dock. Muscular forearms protrude from the rolled-up sleeves of his brown canvas work shirt. A wide smile plays across his face. He navigates the side of the boat to a wooden ladder that extends from the side of the dock into the water. One foot on a ladder rung and the other planted in the middle of the boat, he leans down and ties the rope to a small cleat affixed to the bow of the vessel. It bobs aggressively when the weight of his foot pushes off to climb the ladder's few steps.

"You're late," she says accusingly, but her tone is light, playful.

"Forgive me?" the rower asks, tilting his head up. From under the cap, his brown eyes wrap the girl in an admiring gaze.

"Yes." She reaches out to take hold of his hands, which rise to meet hers. As their fingers touch, the pair disappears.

Chapter Seven

The cell phone alarm pierced the early morning silence. Makenzie fumbled for the offending rectangle on the edge of the nightstand and tapped snooze, then snuggled in the cozy warmth of her down-filled sleeping bag and drifted back to sleep. Five minutes later, a second alarm sounded, prompting Makenzie to throw open her bag to let in the morning chill—a technique that helped her wake up.

Her eyelids fluttered open, the synapses of her brain beginning to fire. Images of the early morning dream played in her mind like a movie reel. The girl dressed in vintage clothing meeting up with a young man at the Baldwin Manor boat dock. Then vanishing.

My interest in the history of the Baldwin Manor from yesterday's tour must have burrowed into my subconscious. I'm sure those ghost stories last night didn't help either.

Makenzie yawned and stretched her arms overhead, noticing the ring on her finger. The stone was aquamarine in the cabin's soft morning light. A complete change from its deep sapphire colour the night before. She gazed at the heart shape, admiring the sea glass hue. It reminded her of the lake's shallow waters, before the depths morphed to a darker indigo blue. *I wonder what makes the colour change?*

A sharp knock on the cabin door interrupted her thoughts. She sat up quickly, burying her hand in the folds of the sleeping bag.

"Come in," Makenzie said, flustered. She watched the knob turn, followed by the creak of the door's metal hinges as it swung open.

"Morning, sunshine," Hannah said with a bright smile, entering the cabin. "Checking to see if you're up."

"I am," Makenzie answered, her hand still hidden. "Barely."

"Breakfast will be ready soon. Meet me at the Chuck House?"

"Yep. I'll see you there."

"Don't be late."

"I won't," Makenzie said.

The breath she was holding escaped in a relieved rush when Hannah closed the door behind her. Makenzie threw the weight of her body down, head cushioned by the pillow.

That was close.

She removed the ring and dropped it in the outside pocket of her backpack, then zipped the small compartment, hiding the band from Hannah and her guilty conscience.

The clang of the triangle sounded throughout the camp just as Makenzie stepped out of the girl's bathhouse into the cool morning air. The mouthwatering aroma of bacon teased her stomach, which responded with a growl. She followed the dusty path to the Chuck House. Rumour had it that campers named it long ago after a grouchy but kind cook who grumbled under his breath about having to work for a bunch of bratty kids. But then spent his time off making chocolate chip cookies for their weekly hike.

Makenzie walked through the open door of the Chuck House, stopping to search for Hannah who was seated at one of the long metal tables, chatting with Naomi. Makenzie waved, catching Hannah's attention, eliciting a head nod in response. She grabbed a grey plastic tray and a plate, then loaded it with a heaping spoonful of steaming scrambled eggs, thick bacon slices, and a pile of buttered toast.

"Hungry, are we?" Hannah teased, noticing Makenzie's overflowing plate.

"Starved." Makenzie took a bite of bacon, savouring the hickory taste as she chewed.

"It's going to be busy today with campers arriving this afternoon," Hannah said. "But it'll be fun too, meeting the girls who'll be in your cabin for the week."

"I hope I don't get a homesick kid," Naomi said. "Last year, there was a camper who wasn't ready to be away from home. We had to sleep with the lights on the whole week." Naomi rolled her eyes. "Some of the girls made fun of her, which didn't help."

Makenzie listened intently as she devoured her breakfast. She couldn't imagine being homesick. Maybe if she was younger, but she was thankful to be away from her parents and their overprotectiveness.

"That happened to me once," Hannah said knowingly. "Mrs. White has night lights if it happens again. Just go ask her for one."

"Good to know," Makenzie said, her words barely audible through a mouthful of half-eaten toast. Relaxed moments before, the girl's conversation made Makenzie apprehensive about camp starting. She dropped the remaining piece of toast on her plate while her full stomach did a nervous somersault.

Mrs. White stood at the front of the Chuck House, loudly tapping her coffee mug with a spoon to get the attention of the noisy group.

"Good morning, Camp Baldwin counsellors," she said enthusiastically.

"Good morning, Mrs. White," the group fired back in a singsong cadence punctuated with smiling faces.

"It's great to hear your excitement on our first day of camp. You've all worked hard preparing for today. Thank you for getting the camp ready for the summer. Registration begins at 2:00, but there are always a few anxious families who arrive early. Please meet at the registration table at 1:30 so you can greet your campers when they get here. And don't forget to wear your name tag."

Mrs. White bent her neck forward, looking down at the front of her chest.

"I guess that goes for me too," she chuckled, noticing the absent wooden disk. "There's one more housekeeping item I forgot to mention. Between meals and snack time, no one should be hungry, but just in case, there'll always be a bowl of fruit and granola bars just inside the door of the Chuck House after dinner so you can grab a quick bite if you need something to tide you over until morning. Any questions?"

Mrs. White scanned the group for raised hands, eyes peering out above the glasses perched at the end of her nose.

"Alright then. Come pick up your cabin roster when I call your name. Alex."

While she listened for her name to be called, Makenzie's thoughts turned to the ring. Safely hidden in her backpack, she could leave it there all summer and start wearing it when she got home. But there was something about it, maybe the way the stone changed colour, that intrigued her.

"Makenzie," Mrs. White said, glancing in her direction.

Makenzie stood to retrieve her list of campers, sure her face was flushed. As if Mrs. White could read her thoughts about the stashed ring and the broken rule.

"Thanks," Makenzie mumbled to Mrs. White when she took the list, then darted out of the Chuck House.

Makenzie walked along the path to the Baldwin Manor boat dock, mindful of Hannah's suggestion that cell phone service was better there.

She paused when Lake Tahoe came into view, taking in its natural beauty. The sea glass hued water near the beach was so clear she could see the rocks below. The colour changed from teal to indigo the farther out her eyes travelled. Shimmers of light from the sun's reflection danced on the mirror-like surface. She swiped her phone out of her back pocket and tapped it open.

"Hi, Jess. How's it going?"

"Hey, stranger. It's going fine. I haven't heard from you since you left. I thought you forgot about me," Jessica said coolly.

"I think about you all the time and wish you were here. We've been busy getting the camp ready for today. The first week of campers arrive this afternoon. I wanted to call before things get hectic."

"Gee, thanks. Who is we?" Jessica asked, an edge to her voice.

"All the counsellors. I've been paired up with Hannah, a Tahoe local. It's her second summer as a counsellor. All the first years were matched with a buddy to help learn the ins and outs of camp. She's super nice, Jess. You'd really like her."

"Glad to hear you've got a new friend," Jessica quipped.

Captivated by the changing colours of the water, Makenzie didn't pick up on her best friend's sarcasm.

"I found this really beautiful ring in the lake. It's gold with a heart-shaped stone that changes colour sometimes," Makenzie said, leaving out Hannah's prompting to turn it in.

"That's cool. Text me a pic."

"Okay, give me a sec." Makenzie reached into her front pocket to retrieve the band, then slipped it on her finger. "I'm putting you on speaker." She tapped the phone. "Still there?"

"Yeah." Jessica's voice floated into the air.

Makenzie opened the phone's camera, held her hand up, and took a couple pictures. It was awkward with one hand, but she managed. With a few quick taps on the screen, she texted the photos to Jessica.

"Did you get them?" Makenzie took the ring off and returned it to its hiding place.

"You found that? Wow! It's beautiful."

"I know. Crazy, huh? A nice souvenir from the summer."

"Really nice. What's that big building in the background?" Jessica asked.

"It's the Baldwin Manor. Remember, this year is its 100th Anniversary. Counsellors are helping with the celebration events at the end of the summer."

"Well, you are. I'm stuck here," Jessica said, her tone sullen.

"That reminds me. I had the strangest dream. A girl dressed in old-fashioned clothing was standing on the dock in front of the manor. Then a guy rowed up in a paddle boat. His clothes were old-fashioned too. He got out of the boat and stood on the dock with the girl. They said a few things I don't remember. And then they disappeared."

"That's weird," Jessica said. "But dreams can be that way."

"I know. I think it was because some counsellors were telling ghost stories around the campfire last night. It was really fun. We made s'mores."

Jessica was silent.

"You still there, Jess?" Makenzie asked.

"I gotta go, Kenzie. Glad you're having a good time. Bye," Jessica said quietly, then hung up.

Chapter Eight

Makenzie stood in the parking lot, her body tingling with nervous anticipation while she waited for her first camper to arrive. She secretly hoped none of the girls bunking in her cabin would be homesick, at least not during the first week.

As Mrs. White predicted, cars snaked down the camp's long drive well before 2:00, their excited occupants wanting to check in early to snag a top bunk before their less seasoned cabinmates arrived. Makenzie's first camper, Avery, was part of this group. A bubbly 10-year-old who proudly announced this was her third year at Camp Baldwin. She'd also bunked in Pinewood before so her parents escorted her there, letting Makenzie wait at registration to greet the rest of the week's campers.

Makenzie was exhausted when the triangle finally sounded for dinner. The repeated trekking back and forth to Pinewood, combined with reassuring concerned parents their daughters would have a great week, began to wear on her by the time the last girl on her roster arrived. Hannah was no help. She had been busy meeting her six campers and getting them settled.

If only Jess was here. The afternoon had been so hectic, Makenzie didn't realize how much she missed her. Sure, she'd be doing the same thing with her own cabin full of girls, but at least they'd be doing it together. *It's not like Jess to hang up so quickly,* Makenzie thought, reflecting on their call. *I didn't even ask how she's doing. I hope her leg is healing.* She promised herself to check in with her best friend soon.

"What's with the long face?" Hannah said, plopping her tray on the table across from Makenzie as she sat down on the wooden bench to join her.

"Oh, hey," Makenzie said, jolted out of her thoughts. "Just tired I guess, long day." She didn't feel like telling Hannah about her conversation with Jess. She was getting good at hiding things. Including the ring nestled in the fabric of her front pocket.

"I get it. The first day can be overwhelming. It'll get easier." Hannah grabbed the burger off her plate and took a huge bite, smiling while she chewed. "Delish," she said, after swallowing. "How are your campers?"

"Good so far. One girl, Avery, has been here before. The rest are first-timers. They seem like sweet girls."

"You say that now, but wait until after s'mores tonight when they're all tired, but hopped up on sugar." Hannah flashed a wicked grin.

"Really, Hannah, how bad can it be?" Makenzie said with a smile, weariness fading with each bite.

"Trust me. Just remember, you're the counsellor," Hannah said. Her green eyes drilled into Makenzie for emphasis. "Don't let them talk you into staying up late. Lights out is at 9:30."

"Okay, okay," Makenzie said, with a chuckle. "Thanks for the advice."

"That's what I'm here for," Hannah said lightly.

Hannah was spot on. Being excited and worn out from their first day, mixed with sugary s'mores at the end of the evening, was a recipe for shenanigans. Makenzie was hesitant at first about putting an end to the girl's fun, but it had gotten out of hand. Silly jokes and laughter were okay, but the pillow fight and yelling that ensued wasn't.

The following morning, Avery, who had quickly become Pinewood's spokesperson, sidled next to Makenzie as the campers and counsellors stood in front of the Baldwin Manor, waiting for a tour.

"We're really sorry about last night, Makenzie," Avery said, looking up at her with a timid smile. "We promise it won't happen again."

Makenzie glanced over at Avery's cabinmates who stood together quietly a few feet away, solemn expressions on their young faces. "Thank you, Avery. Apology accepted." She grinned down at the girl's relieved face. "I'm sure it won't." Makenzie looked toward the Pinewood crowd, happy to see their smiles had returned.

The lush green lawn in front of the Baldwin Manor overflowed with the younger half of the camp's occupants. A few counsellors stood guard at the boat dock, ensuring that some of the more playful kids didn't push each other into the lake, which had happened before. At 9:00 sharp, the glass-panelled double doors of the manor opened and Mrs. White, followed by Thomas, walked to the edge of the wide, wooden front porch to address the waiting group.

"Happy Monday. I hope everyone had a good night's sleep," Mrs. White announced, looking out over the crowd. Makenzie caught Avery's eye and gave her a playful wink.

"In keeping with tradition, the first morning of camp is a tour of the Baldwin Manor," the camp director continued. "This is Thomas Flint, the property's caretaker and historian. He oversees summer tours, along with the museum and gift shop."

Thomas acknowledged the group with a quick wave. He appeared more relaxed than when Makenzie first met him in the garden, but remained unsmiling.

"We'll break into two groups for the tour. Those of you in cabins Emerald, Tuscarora, Silver Dollar, and Baldwin will be stuck with me." Mrs. White paused, giving the crowd a lighthearted smile. "Pinewood, Aurora, Richardson, and Sugar Pine campers will go with Mr. Flint. If you're in my group, head over to the boat dock. Mr. Flint's group will hang out here. We'll start in five."

After more than five minutes of chaos, the campers quieted down, allowing their tour leaders to begin. Makenzie was thankful to be in Thomas' group. The tour Mrs. White gave the counsellors a few days ago was good, but as the historian of the property, she thought Thomas would be more interesting.

"Over the centuries, this site has been a haven for many people. The Washoe Indians were the first to enjoy its serene beauty. They came from the Eastern Sierras to escape the desert heat, gather food, and savour the mountain setting. In the 1870s, scenic Lake Tahoe became a destination, luring people from all over California and beyond," Thomas said to the group crowded around him. His quiet but commanding demeanour captivated his young audience, including Makenzie.

She surveyed the small swath of beach in front of the manor, imagining the thousands of footprints the sand held over time. Thomas' vivid details painted a picture of life in the 1920s when the manor was being built, through its present-day iteration as a historic site. Even though Makenzie was drawn to his stories like a moth to a flame, as Thomas led the group around the manor's various structures, she felt his no-nonsense style of speaking gave off a teacherly vibe. Interesting, but not very personable.

"The 100th Anniversary Celebration at the end of the summer will commemorate the Baldwin family and their gift of the historic manor to the United States Forest Service in the 1960s. The partnership ensured that the property would be preserved throughout time," Thomas said, ending the tour in front of the rustic façade of the Baldwin Manor. "Are there any questions?"

"How come you know so much about when Camp Baldwin was built?" a boy with unruly curls in a faded Star Wars t-shirt asked.

"Well, because I helped build it."

"No way," the boy said, his eyes wide with surprise.

"I was a young man in the 1960s when the camp was constructed," Thomas said. "I liked the outdoors and needed a job."

"That's cool," the boy said.

Makenzie raised her hand. Thomas looked in her direction and gave a nod to speak.

"So what did you do after the camp was completed?"

Thomas shuffled his feet together, seeming to pause. He studied Makenzie intently, like he was contemplating the answer.

"I was hired as the manor's caretaker and took care of the property until it transitioned to the Forest Service. Because I knew so much, they kept me on in various positions over the years. I've worked here most of my life," Thomas stated matter-of-factly. He turned his head to look toward the nearby boat dock.

His brown eyes softened momentarily, shedding his formidable appearance. His expression was melancholy. The loneliness Makenzie saw the first day she met him returned. Then, in a blink of his eye, it was gone.

"That's the end of the tour. Mine tends to run longer than Mrs. White's. It's time for you kids to head back to Camp Baldwin."

Makenzie looked at the vacant dock. Pale turquoise water lapped softly at the piers underneath uniform wood planks that marched out above the lake's surface, forming the boat dock. A small paddle boat was tied to one of the metal cleats that dotted the edge of the dock. *What was it that made Thomas react that way?* She was even more determined to get him to smile.

Chapter Nine

"Hey, Mom. Happy Saturday." Makenzie's tanned legs swayed slowly back and forth, dangling off the side of the Baldwin Manor dock. Her cell phone lay next to her on the worn wood. The white earphones hanging from each ear a stark contrast against her raven black hair.

"Well, hello." Her mother's voice was crisp. "We were beginning to wonder when you'd call."

Makenzie winced. "Sorry, I've been really busy cleaning up the camp and getting used to the routine, in addition to monitoring six campers."

"That's what Mrs. White said when I spoke with her earlier this week."

"You called her to check on me?" Makenzie's legs jerked to a stop. Her whole body tensed. *Unbelievable.* She rolled her eyes at the lake.

"Yes, dear. When we didn't hear from you after a few days, we wanted to make sure everything was okay. That there wasn't a reason why you didn't call. Mrs. White confirmed you were doing well and busy, like you said. I did try calling you, but it went to voicemail."

Makenzie took in a deep breath, trying to remain calm. "Mom, cell phone service is super bad at camp. I had to walk over to the property next door to get good coverage so I could call you. I can't do that when camp is in session."

"I see." There was a brief pause. "Let's make a plan for you to check in once a week. Will that work?"

"Sure," Makenzie said through clenched teeth. "Campers leave Friday morning and arrive again on Sunday afternoon. So, Saturday would be a good day."

"Okay, Saturday it is. Are you enjoying yourself?" Her mother's tone softened.

Enjoying being away from your constant supervision, Makenzie thought, but didn't dare say.

"Yeah. Now that the first week of camp is over, I know the routine. S'mores by the campfire on the first night and the last. On Monday, there's a tour of the Baldwin Manor. The historian who works there reminds me of Grandpa."

"Really? How so?"

"His hair is wavy and white and he has brown eyes and glasses. But he's not funny like Grandpa. He actually seems kinda sad."

"Maybe he has a lot on his mind," Makenzie's mom reasoned.

"Could be. Anyway, campers have arts and crafts on Tuesday and there's a really cool four-mile hike up Zephyr Trail on Wednesday. We take a bag lunch and eat in a meadow at the top of the trail. Thursday is ziplining."

"Sounds like fun, Kenzie. Are you keeping up with your swimming? You know that was one of the reasons we agreed to let you spend the summer there. You promised you'd practice so you don't fall behind."

Makenzie glared at the line of pine trees that shaded the beach across from her. "Yes, Mom. There's swim time every afternoon. I practice then."

"That's good. We miss you."

"Miss you too," Makenzie lied with a grimace she was thankful her mother couldn't see. "How's Dad?"

"Busy with work. He has a business trip to Seattle, so I'm joining him to visit your aunt Meghen for a few days."

Makenzie listened half-heartedly while her mom filled her in on the details of their upcoming trip. Although she was in a completely different state, she still couldn't escape their grasp. It was as if they'd cast an invisible net to keep her under their thumbs.

She looked down and admired the ring. She'd slipped it on before going to bed and hadn't taken it off since Hannah had gone home for the weekend. Its teal blue hue mirrored the water that gently lapped the boat dock pilings underneath her feet.

"So, it will be nice to get away for a few days," her mother said. The sound of her voice knocked Makenzie out of her rambling thoughts and back into their conversation.

"Tell Dad and Aunt Meg I said hello. Have a fun trip."

"I will, honey. Have a good week. I'll talk to you next Saturday. And be good."

"Bye, Mom," Makenzie said, ignoring her last comment. She tapped the phone off and removed her earphones, dropping them in a jumbled pile on the weathered dock.

Will my parents ever understand me? She was doing a good job. Mrs. White had told her as much yesterday. Avery's parents were late picking her up, so she and Makenzie played ping-pong and chatted about the week until they arrived. Mrs. White had thanked her for being dedicated.

A figure walking toward the boathouse interrupted Makenzie's thoughts. She wore a shapeless navy dress that ended a few inches above her ankles. Curious, Makenzie stood, grabbed her phone and earphones, and shoved them in the back pocket of her faded denim shorts. She walked off the dock and headed toward the boathouse. Instinctively, she shoved her right hand in her front pocket to hide the ring, not knowing why. The girl wouldn't know it wasn't truly hers.

As she approached, Makenzie saw the girl enter the boathouse, but she returned seconds later. Closer now, Makenzie realized her dress was from another era. Its crisp white sailor's collar came to a V in the front, completed by a ring of navy fabric that held the collar's two end pieces neatly together. Her long hair was gathered loosely at the back of her neck by a wide navy bow. Simple white canvas shoes completed her outfit.

"Hi," Makenzie said.

"Hello." The girl's bright hazel eyes settled on Makenzie. A slight smile formed on her lips.

"You must be one of the 100th Anniversary Celebration volunteers?"

"What gave me away?" the girl said lightheartedly as she swept her hand in front of her vintage dress.

"My name is Makenzie. I'm a junior counsellor at Camp Baldwin." She pointed toward the camp with her free hand, the other still buried deep in her pocket.

"My friends call me Cody." She pointed to a small wooden box resting on a metal folding chair just outside the structure's door. "Would you like some information about the Baldwin Manor boathouse? Feel free to take one."

"Sure, thanks," Makenzie said, grabbing one of the colourful pamphlets from the box. "I'm surprised at how fascinated I've become with this place. I often wonder what it would've been like to live here in its heyday."

Cody scanned the manor's wood and stone façade. The sparkle in her hazel eyes dulled abruptly, then brightened. "It was interesting."

Makenzie gave her a questioning look.

"From the history I've learned," Cody clarified quickly.

Makenzie nodded. "It was good to meet you. I hope to see you again over the summer."

"I'll be here," Cody said, disappearing through the boathouse door.

Makenzie turned toward camp. As she walked, her hand slipped out of her pocket. She looked down absentmindedly to admire the ring, then stopped. The stone's earlier teal blue shade had morphed to a deep sapphire blue. She wasn't sure, but it felt like the skin under the band tingled.

That's so odd. I wonder what makes it change colour?

Chapter Ten

The bare light bulb dangling from Pinewood's ceiling cast a shiny glare on the sepia image of the Baldwin Manor boathouse. Cuddled up in the warmth of her sleeping bag, Makenzie devoured the pamphlet Cody had given her that morning.

Built in the 1930s, the boathouse barely contained the Baldwin family's 60-foot wooden yacht, the Zephyr. State-of-the-art at the time, the structure was equipped with a motorized winch and launching rails that extended out of the building into Lake Tahoe. The mechanism lifted the boat out of the water, enabling passengers to enter and exit the craft onto a platform without getting their shoes or clothing wet.

Makenzie set the flyer on the nightstand and snuggled deeper into her bag, imagining what life must have been like back then. No power boats or Jet Skis flying across the water, their motors polluting the fresh mountain air with exhaust and noise. What she envisioned was much more serene. Silent vessels crawling at a sea turtle's pace above the cerulean surface. She was surprised at how the glory days of the Baldwin Manor enchanted her. So different from present day life. Not that she'd want to have lived back then. She just enjoyed learning about its history.

On the verge of falling asleep, and not wanting to leave the cozy nest of her sleeping bag, Makenzie talked herself into getting up in the chilly night air to flick off the light switch. One last glance at the ring before the cabin went dark revealed a dark aquamarine heart.

Smiling, the girl steps off the dock. Her booted feet crush the sand at the base of the stairs. She turns away from the dark façade of the Baldwin Manor and waves to the figure standing at the end of the dock. Her bright white blouse glows in the twilight. A young man in a brown shirt waves back. His face is a shadow, formed by the brim of his flat cap.

With one last flick of her wrist, the girl turns away and continues toward the manor. In the crepuscular light, she approaches the wide staircase, grasping handfuls of her long skirt to navigate the steps before her. Porch lights fashioned out of glass and metal flick on abruptly, flooding the girl with light. Illuminated, confusion sets in and her eyes grow wide with fear. She releases the fabric of her skirt as her head tilts up to look at the manor's front door.

One of the twin wood and glass panelled doors swings open abruptly. A man in dark trousers and a jacket with wide lapels charges through the doorway. His lips are set in a thin line below hard, glaring eyes. In a few strides, he reaches the top of the stairs. Hands planted on his hips, he looks down at the girl. Her frightened eyes meet his. She takes a step back, turns, and flees toward the dock.

Makenzie's eyelids snapped open; her heart raced. She sat up to slow the pounding in her chest and grabbed her phone from the corner of the rickety nightstand—3:43 a.m. Her eyes skimmed the cover of the boathouse flyer as she set the glowing rectangle down. *The manor's history must have crept into my subconscious. Why else would I dream about it again? So weird. And what's with the girl?*

Makenzie thought back to her first peculiar dream. *I'm sure it's the same girl.* Heartbeat slowed, she plopped her head on the soft flannel of her pillowcase and burrowed into the comforting warmth of her sleeping bag. "Just a dream, Kenzie," she said aloud to soothe herself, before closing her eyes. *It doesn't mean anything.* But it took a while for her to fall back to sleep.

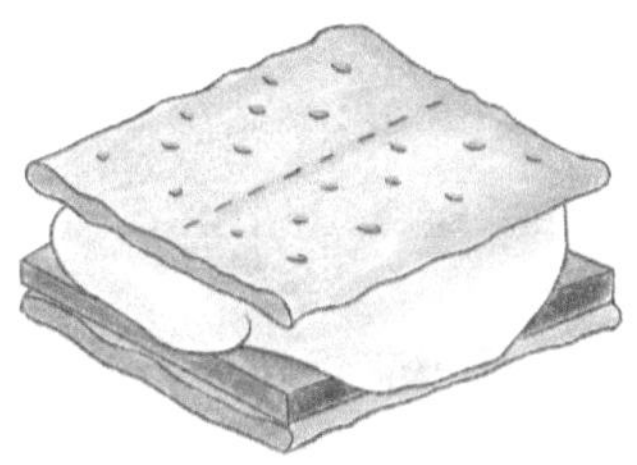

Chapter Eleven

It only took a couple of weeks for Makenzie to get the hang of the camp's easy-going routine. Sunday afternoons brought a new group of Pinewood girls, which she enjoyed getting to know during their five-day stay in the cabin. Each shared their unique personality and appreciated her as their counsellor. All except one camper who was a troublemaker from day one. Makenzie was glad that week was behind her.

The short weekend break between camp sessions was a fun respite. Makenzie loved being able to sleep in and just chill out, unless there was a project Mrs. White wanted them to complete. Even then, it was fun because they were all working together. Like when they organized the arts and crafts closet in the Zephyr Lodge.

On one memorable afternoon, Hannah's crush, Alex, discovered a box of old squirt guns tucked away in a corner shelf. He filled one to see if they still worked. When it did, everyone joined in, which led to a commando-style squirt gun fight amidst the trees. Luckily, Mrs. White had a sense of humour that day.

Long afternoons at the beach were Makenzie's favourite. After swim practice, she'd lounge with Hannah, the duo sprawled out on colourful towels in the sand; or, if Hannah had gone home to spend time with her family, she'd hang out with Naomi.

Makenzie was elated to be out from under the watchful eyes of her parents. Her independence at Camp Baldwin was even better than she'd imagined. Other than talking with them once a week when she checked in, she felt free as a bird; her heart light as a feather.

"Hey, Dad," Makenzie said. Legs crossed, she was perched at the edge of the Baldwin Manor dock after a long morning swim.

"Hi, kiddo, we hoped you'd call."

"It's Saturday, isn't it?" Makenzie said, a little too irritably. Just the sound of her father's voice put her in defence mode.

"Yep. How's it going? Are you finding time to swim?"

Makenzie felt her stomach cave in as her muscles tightened, involuntarily reacting to his over-parenting.

"Camp is fine, Dad. And yes, I just finished a long swim." She emphasized the word "just."

"Good. Remember, that was one of our agreements for you to go away for the summer."

"I know." Makenzie sighed. "I'm swimming almost every day. Probably more than if I was at home. How's Mom?" she asked, changing the subject.

"She's fine. She misses you. I do too."

"Miss you guys too," Makenzie said, not really feeling it. "How was Seattle?"

She half-heartedly listened to the details of her parent's trip. Reprimanded and missed at the same time. Her father's contrasting comments cast a dark cloud of guilt over her heart.

Do I miss my parents? Her eyes scanned the indigo water as though its depths held the answers to her jumbled feelings.

"Aunt Meg says hello," her dad said, grabbing Makenzie's attention and eliciting a smile. Single with no kids, her Aunt Meg had always treated her like a grown-up, even when she was younger.

"How's my favourite aunt?"

"Doing well. She thinks it's great you're spending the summer away at camp," her dad answered.

"Really? I should send her a postcard."

"Will we get one too?"

"Sure, Dad," Makenzie said, her mood improved. "I'll talk to you next week."

"Bye, Kenzie. Love you."

"Love you too."

Makenzie tapped her phone off. She did love her parents, just not their long-distance supervision. She was holding up her end of their summer bargain, keeping up with her swimming so she'd be ready to compete when meets started in the fall.

Reaching into her backpack, she pulled out a tube of sunscreen, and applied the white lotion on her tanned legs and feet while thoughts of home swirled in her head. Because it was in the upper 80s, she threw on her short-sleeved swim shirt to prevent her back from getting sunburned. *If only Jess were here. She'd time my swim practice during weekend breaks. And help with sunscreen.* She swiped the tube across her forearm, leaving a line of coconut-scented cream, which she rubbed in before tapping Jessica's number in her contacts.

"It's about time you called."

"How's it going?" Makenzie's feet dangled off the side of the boat dock. In the distance, she watched tourists mill about the manor's façade, taking photos and stopping to read inscriptions embedded in the historical placards scattered about the property.

"It's going. I'm so done with this cast. It's really hard to sleep in, so I'm tired all the time. Josh felt sorry for me and took me to a movie last night."

"Impressive. That was a nice big brother thing to do," Makenzie said.

"It was. I think my mom put him up to it. But it got me out of the house and kept me from feeling sorry for myself for a couple hours anyway."

"How's your leg? Is it healing?"

"Slowly. Next week they'll remove the cast and X-ray from the knee down to see how the bones are mending. Hopefully I can start physical therapy soon."

"That'd be great, Jess. Then you'll have more to keep you busy."

"How's camp?"

"Really good. Campers are excited to be here which makes it fun. The hiking and ziplining days make the week fly by. Then there's down time on the weekends where it's just the counsellors. I spend a lot of it swimming. Sometimes there's a movie in the Zephyr Lodge."

"Glad you're having a good time. How's your new friend? What's her name, Heather?"

"Hannah," Makenzie corrected. "She went home for the weekend. Her older sister is back from college and she wanted to spend time with her."

"How nice," Jessica said. Not very nicely.

"I had another strange dream. This time the girl in vintage clothing was scared. She ran away from a man coming out of the Baldwin Manor."

"Creepy," Jess said. The word was clipped.

"I think so too. The history of this place is really interesting. Maybe it's taken over my dreams," Makenzie thought out loud. "But I doubt it means anything."

"I gotta go, Kenz. Talk to you later."

The phone clicked off before Makenzie could say goodbye.

Chapter Twelve

What was that about? Makenzie stared at her phone as if it would give her an answer. *Where did Jess have to go?* Although it was done politely, her best friend had just hung up on her.

Makenzie swallowed hard, trying to digest her hurt feelings. She looked out at the lake. Its calm reflection conflicted with her inner turmoil. *If Jess is having a hard time sleeping because of the cast, maybe she's just grouchy*, Makenzie reasoned. *And she's stuck at home for the summer. Two really good reasons to be irritated. And I'm telling her what a great time I'm having. No wonder she had to go.*

Makenzie tapped the message icon under Jessica's number and started typing. *I'm really sorry about your leg and the summer. Wish you were here.* A sad face emoji punctuated the end of the text.

Dots danced on Makenzie's screen. *Thx,* followed by a purple heart emoji.

The breath Makenzie didn't realize she was holding escaped. Her chest felt lighter. *Jess wasn't upset.* A smile replaced her worried frown.

Makenzie stood and grabbed her beach towel, dry now from the morning sun. Although Hannah was home for the weekend, Makenzie was excited about the afternoon. Naomi and a few of the other counsellors had invited her to hike the Zephyr Cove Trail after lunch. Makenzie tapped her phone. Imposed in white numbers over the screen saver shot of her and Jessica was the time. 12:30. She'd need to hurry if she wanted to make it to the Chuck House before lunch ended. She slung her backpack over her shoulder, slipped on her flip-flops, and jogged toward the Baldwin Manor boat dock stairs.

The crowds of tourists that flocked to the historic property were in full force. Even more so due to the 100th anniversary events taking place throughout the summer. Visitors flitted from structure to structure, stopping to learn about its unique past from docents dressed in clothing of the bygone era.

Makenzie delighted in watching the days of old come to life. On the lawn in front of the school room, a woman in a white three-quarter sleeved shirt, pleats running up the front, held an abacus. Belted at the waist, her long black skirt stopped just above dark boots that laced up the front. The woman's hair was neatly gathered under a short-brimmed straw hat, festooned with a wide scarlet ribbon. A thin black tie hung from the shirt's stiff collar, completing her scholarly outfit.

The contrast between the short-wearing tourists and the docent's vintage clothing made for great people-watching. At the boathouse, Cody, clad in her retro navy dress, waved at her from inside the structure's open doorway. Makenzie smiled and waved back. Stepping off the dock, she saw Thomas standing on the beach nearby, looking down at the clear water.

"Hi, Mr. Flint," Makenzie said, walking toward him. "Did you lose something?"

Thomas lifted his head to look at her. After a few seconds, a spark of recognition flickered in his eyes.

"You're at Camp Baldwin, correct?"

"Yes. Makenzie Taylor. I'm a junior counsellor. I really like your tours. I learn something new every time."

"That's nice to hear."

Makenzie detected a hint of pleasure in his monotone reply. She'd gotten used to his expressionless way of talking from the various historical descriptions he shared with the campers.

"I'm giving one soon. Just passing time until it starts."

"So, you didn't lose anything?" Makenzie repeated, noticing his gaze had returned to the clear water gently lapping over the shoreline's golden sand.

After a long pause, as if he was thinking how to answer her

question, Thomas replied, "I lost something here a long time ago. Something I'll never get back." Sadness emanated from his words. He lifted his head and glanced toward the boat dock. His sorrowful eyes lingered there briefly before returning to scan the lake.

Makenzie was taken aback. Surprised by his openness, she wasn't sure how to respond. "Umm, I'm late meeting some of the other counsellors for a hike. See you around."

"See you," Thomas said, his eyes still focused on the water.

The glow of dancing flames cast a faint orange tint on Makenzie's profile as she studied the marshmallow turning golden brown on the long metal roasting stick she twirled slowly over the fire. Overhead, the full moon cast a pale light on the small group of counsellors gathered around the fire ring.

"I'm beat," Naomi said. "Today's hike was way longer than when we go with the kids on Wednesdays." She sat across from Makenzie, staring as if mesmerized by the flickering orange-red of the flame.

"Yeah, but it was fun. The view of the lake at the top of the trail is amazing."

Satisfied the puffy marshmallow was ready, Makenzie plucked it off the stick, blew on it a few times, and took a bite.

"Delish!"

"I can hardly keep my eyes open. My sleeping bag is calling. You coming?" Naomi asked Makenzie, who had grabbed another marshmallow from the almost empty bowl.

"Just one more."

"Okay. Do you want my flashlight?" Naomi asked. "Maybe you should have grabbed yours."

Makenzie looked up at the full moon. The luminous orb cast a faint light over the fire pit and nearby trees.

"I'll be able to get back without it. Thanks though."

"See you in the morning. Make sure the Baldwin Manor ghost doesn't get you."

"I don't believe in ghosts, remember?" Makenzie said, twisting the puffy square onto the end of the metal stick.

"I remember." Naomi followed the beam of her flashlight down the rock-lined path toward Cabin Row. "Waaaa haaaa haaaa," she cackled into the night.

"Very funny," Makenzie hollered with a laugh.

When the marshmallow was coated in a brown caramelized crust, Makenzie devoured it like she hadn't eaten all day. In response, her stomach gurgled. *How am I hungry? Must be the combo of my morning swim and afternoon hike. Eating all this sugar isn't helping.*

Makenzie remembered the fruit and granola bars Mrs. White mentioned would be available in the Chuck House if counsellors needed a snack. She'd seen the bowl on a small table by the door. Thinking she would sleep better with some real food in her belly,

Makenzie started up the path that led to the Chuck House.

The bright moonlight made it easy for Makenzie to navigate the wide path through the scattered pines. Bathed in its luminescence, a feeling of calm washed over her.

Moths danced around a pair of rustic light fixtures mounted on the front of the wooden building. Their wide circular glow threw light into the Chuck House when Makenzie opened the door. She grabbed a banana and some granola bars to stash in her backpack for later. Slipping the bars in the front pocket of her Camp Baldwin hoodie, Makenzie peeled the banana and took a bite as she walked toward Cabin Row.

It was different walking through the camp at night. With no noisy campers and many of the counsellors gone for the weekend, it was unusually quiet. Makenzie finished the fruit and tossed the peel in a garbage can near the Zephyr Lodge. Now that her rumbling stomach was appeased, all she wanted was to wrap herself in the warmth of her sleeping bag. It had been a long day.

A swirl of clouds covered the moon when Makenzie walked away from the well-lit façade of Zephyr Lodge, leaving her in the dark. In the distance, she could see the steady incandescent porch lights that dotted the structures of Cabin Row. The sudden darkness, coupled with being alone, gave Makenzie the creeps. The peaceful quiet had morphed into an eerie silence. Her heart started beating faster. Alert now, eyes focused on the lights ahead, she quickened her pace.

Makenzie practically ran into the girls' bathhouse at the edge of Cabin Row. The safety of its bright overhead lights was a welcome relief. She grinned at her reflection in the long mirror that hung above half-a-dozen chrome sinks. *What a goof. Scared by a little darkness.* She grabbed her toothbrush from the wooden storage shelf opposite the mirror and brushed, calmed by the nightly routine.

Finished in the bathhouse, Makenzie walked leisurely toward Pinewood. The clouds had dissipated, allowing the moonlight to shine down on Cabin Row. She yawned, the day's activities catching up with her.

As she climbed the few worn stairs leading to Pinewood, a movement down by the beach caught her attention. Makenzie stopped to look, straining to make out what it was. *Probably some of the older counsellors walking on the beach.* Which was off limits after dark. Another camp rule.

Tired, but curious, Makenzie turned and walked back down the stairs. She headed toward the beach, the light of the moon guiding her way along the path. In the distance, the moon's reflection shimmered on the still lake.

When she reached the end of the dirt path, Makenzie surveyed the sandy beach. Nothing. *Must have been my imagination, or the moonlight playing tricks on me.* She gazed at the luminescent water for a moment, then turned to head back.

Out of the corner of her eye, Makenzie glimpsed a phosphorescent glow near the Baldwin Manor. Her eyes grew wide and her heart skipped a beat. She felt the chill of goosebumps run up her arms. Not wanting to, but needing to know, Makenzie turned, squinting to get a better look. It was a silhouette. She gasped, her hands reaching up to cover her mouth.

The figure turned toward her, then disappeared.

Chapter Thirteen

Heart beating like a drum, Makenzie sprinted to Pinewood. She ran up the steps, flicked on the light switch, and locked the door behind her. Throwing herself on the bed, she grabbed her pillow and hugged it tight. After several deep breaths, her pounding heart slowed.

What was that? A trick of the moonlight? Someone playing a joke? A camper who wasn't supposed to be there? Makenzie's thoughts raced, trying to rationalize what it was she saw.

A trespasser who didn't want to get caught? That could be. Thomas locks up the area surrounding the manor when it closes at dusk, but someone could still get in if they really wanted to. Or was it the Baldwin Manor ghost? That story Alex told when camp started about counsellors seeing a girl at night who disappears.

Although Makenzie's hoodie was warm, a sudden chill crawled down her spine. She twisted her back a couple of times, shaking off the unwanted feeling. *I don't believe in ghosts. They're just made-up tales to scare people.* That's what her parents told her when she was little and frightened by a trick of the light or a spooky TV show. Like the monsters she imagined lived under her bed, waiting to come out in the middle of the night. Not real.

Makenzie changed into her flannel PJs and turned off the light. The soft shine of moonlight imprinted a square on the floor through the window's thin fabric curtain, giving her some comfort in the dark. Even though she was exhausted, her overactive thoughts wouldn't let her sleep. She replayed the scary scene over and over until she convinced herself it was somebody trespassing on the manor grounds who didn't want to get caught. That's why they disappeared. The light she saw was probably from their flashlight. Satisfied with her theory, Makenzie finally fell asleep.

Sitting in the weathered Adirondack chair on Pinewood's small porch addressing postcards, Makenzie smiled when she looked up to see Hannah standing in front of the cabin.

"Welcome back. How was the weekend with your family?"

"Awesome. I hung out with my sister and our dad took us water skiing. What'd you do?"

Makenzie hesitated. *Should I say anything about last night?* She decided not to. *It was just a trespasser.*

"Swim practice, of course, and a few of us went on a long hike. Mrs. White let us make s'mores last night," Makenzie said, smacking her lips. "Delish as always. I'm sending postcards home to make my parents happy. And my friend Jess."

"The doting daughter," Hannah teased.

Makenzie cringed. "Not really. I do miss my parents. Just not their parenting. Do your mom and dad check up on you all the time? Wanting to know almost every detail about what you're doing?"

Hannah tilted her head. Her green eyes bored into a nearby pine tree as if she'd find the answer to the question there. Shaking her head, she looked back at Makenzie.

"No. By time I came along they were pretty chill. I'm sure my older sister received all the first kid parenting paranoia. You can find out for yourself though."

"What do you mean?"

"Would you be up for staying at my house in a couple weeks? I'll be at camp this coming weekend because my parents are out of town, but the weekend after that, I asked if you could hang out."

"Really? That would be awesome." Makenzie's heart raced with excitement. Then slowed. "I'll have to ask my parents though."

"Maybe Mrs. White could help. Reassure them my family is okay," Hannah suggested. "She's known us for years. Remember, my sister was a counsellor here in high school."

"That just might work. I'll check in with them this week."

"How are you, dear?" Makenzie's mother's words flooded her headphones. It was odd how just the sound of her voice could make Makenzie feel like she was back home, under her watchful eye. It made her even more grateful to be away for the summer, untethered from her parents.

"Great, Mom. I just finished a long swim."

"That's good. I hope you've been able to practice every day?"

Makenzie rolled her eyes. "Just about. I think I'm getting faster, but it could just be the cold water."

"Coach Reynolds will be impressed if that's the case."

"Yep, she will." Makenzie took in a deep breath, crossed her fingers, and hoped for the best. She exhaled then continued. "Remember when I told you about my friend, Hannah? My counsellor mentor for the summer?"

"I remember."

"She's invited me to spend the weekend at her house next week. Her parents said it was okay. They'll be there, along with her sister who's home from college."

"I don't think so, Kenzie. We've never met her family. You know our rule. We need to know your friend's parents. That's a big ask."

Prepared for this exact response, Makenzie put her defensive tactic into play. "Mrs. White can vouch for Hannah and her family. She's known them for a long time. Hannah's sister was a counsellor here. Please, Mom. I really want to go."

Silence filled Makenzie's earphones. "Mom?"

"I'm here. Just thinking. This wasn't part of the summer plan."

"I know. But you'd like Hannah, and Jess isn't here for me to hang out with on the weekends when most of the counsellors go home to be with their families. That wasn't part of the plan either," Makenzie said offensively. Irritation dripped from her words.

Her mother sighed. "No, it wasn't. I'll talk to your dad. If he agrees, we'll check in with Mrs. White."

"That's a lot of ifs," Makenzie fired back, her chest tight with frustration.

"If you want an answer now, it'll be no. I said I'd talk to your father."

"Okay, Mom, thanks." Makenzie backed off, hopeful her dad would be receptive to her request. Her parent's expectation that she behaved had been met. Surely that would weigh in her favour.

She looked down at the ring on her tanned finger. In the morning light, its sky blue stone mirrored the lake's surface. The gnawing guilt she'd felt when she decided to keep it had faded in just a few weeks. Whoever lost it would never know the ring had been found. Her biggest challenge was keeping it hidden from Hannah. She had to stop putting the band on at night, since she kept forgetting to take it off the following morning—the reason why she was admiring it now.

"Give us some time to sort this out. In the meantime, what are you up to this weekend?"

Makenzie took in a breath, accepting she wasn't getting an answer right away. She held on to the slim chance they'd agree and buried her irritation.

"Hannah is staying at camp and tonight all the counsellors get to watch *Beetlejuice* in the Zephyr Lodge. And I'll be swimming, of course."

"Sounds fun."

"It will be. I'm late meeting up with Hannah. Thanks for talking to Dad."

"You're welcome, kiddo. We love you."

"Love you too, Mom."

Makenzie tapped her phone, ending the call. She stared out at the lake, allowing the tightness in her chest to subside. Her mom's lack of a decision was a huge bummer. Now she had to wait for an answer, and it might be no. She didn't like uncertainty.

A movement at the boathouse caught her eye. Cody, in her navy dress, stood in front of the structure's wooden door. Makenzie stood, wrapped her towel into a ball, and shoved it in her backpack. Although she was late meeting Hannah at the Chuck House, she wanted to say hi. The older girl intrigued her. Enamoured with the history of the Baldwin Manor, Makenzie thought it was cool Cody was helping keep its past alive. She wriggled into her shorts and slipped her phone and headphones in the back pocket. She glided her feet into her flip-flops and hurried off the dock.

"You're up early," Cody said with a smile when Makenzie approached the boathouse.

"I just finished swim practice. How's the volunteering? You always look busy when I walk by."

"It's slow in the morning, as you can see." Cody gestured at the short path that connected the boathouse to the Baldwin Manor. A lone squirrel ran across the lush lawn and scrambled up a pine tree. "But there are lots of visitors in the afternoons, so the time flies by." Cody studied Makenzie's eyes under her furrowed brow. "What's with the long face?"

Makenzie grinned sheepishly, thinking she'd left her angst at the dock. "Oh, just frustrated with my parents. They have to approve everything I do. It's so annoying. I wish they'd let me make my own decisions."

Cody nodded in agreement, then shifted her gaze toward the Baldwin Manor. The sparkle in her eyes muted and the lines of her mouth flattened, her thoughts somewhere else. Then her eyes brightened and her smile returned. "My parents were that way too," Cody said.

"My friend Hannah says it's their job," Makenzie said, remembering she was late meeting her at the Chuck House. "Nice to see you. I've got to get back to camp before they stop serving breakfast."

"Hope to see you again," Cody said with a wave.

Makenzie's empty stomach rumbled, encouraging her to pick up the pace. She grabbed her phone from her back pocket to check the time. She'd barely make it back for breakfast. Makenzie glimpsed her hand as it grasped the width of the phone. She stopped. The ring's sky blue colour had transformed to a vibrant indigo. *So weird how it does that.*

Makenzie slipped the band off and shoved it deep into her front pocket, relieved she'd caught her mistake in time before meeting Hannah. She broke into a jog, forgetting her promise to call Jess.

Chapter Fourteen

"Hand me the Scrabble lid." Makenzie pointed behind Hannah to the cardboard box top that lay abandoned across the arm of a faded sofa.

"Whoever was here last sure left a mess," Hannah complained, plucking lettered wooden tiles off the floor of the game nook. She grabbed the lid and dropped the squares into the box before handing it to Makenzie. They were almost finished tidying the Zephyr Lodge, their Saturday camp clean-up assignment.

"Yeah, but at least it was a competitive game," Makenzie said, reading the entwined words "quixotic" and "extreme" that snaked through the middle of the game board. They vanished in a river of squares when she picked up the board, bent it at the centre crease, and waterfalled the tiles back into the box.

"Good, you're still here," Mrs. White said, walking into the lodge. "How's the clean-up going?"

"Almost done. The game nook was a mess," Makenzie answered. She returned the time-worn Scrabble box to a shelf overflowing with games and puzzles.

"Well it's tidy now." The camp director nodded approvingly at Makenzie. "I just got off the phone with your mom."

Makenzie's relaxed muscles stiffened. "Oh-oh," she stammered. "Why?"

"She wanted to know about Hannah's family. Asked if I thought it would be okay for you to spend the weekend," Mrs. White said.

"And?" Hopeful anticipation loosened the tightness that ran the length of Makenzie's spine.

"After a long conversation where I vouched for the Baileys, who I've known for years," Mrs. White paused for emphasis, "your mother said, 'Yes.'"

An excited grin replaced Makenzie's worried frown. "Really?"

"Really." Mrs. White smiled. Makenzie's enthusiasm was contagious.

"Great news, Mrs. W," Hannah chimed in for Makenzie, who was temporarily speechless.

"Yes, thanks," Makenzie said, recovering. "I don't know what you said, but I'm super grateful."

"I simply told the truth. Hannah's family is wonderful. Anyone they consider a friend is lucky."

Hannah's cheeks turned a rosy shade under her suntan.

"Glad I was able to deliver the good news, and thanks for the clean-up," Mrs. White said. "See you girls at dinner."

Makenzie spat a mouthful of toothpaste in the bathhouse sink then continued brushing, mulling over the day's events while she completed the mindless chore. The frustration she'd felt with her mom was replaced by anticipation for the weekend ahead. She was thankful Mrs. White had persuaded her parents to let her stay at Hannah's. *If only I could master that elusive skill. My life would be so much easier.* She smiled at her mirrored reflection above the sink.

"Checking yourself out, are we?" Hannah teased, walking into the bathhouse. She plopped her purple toiletry bag on the counter.

Makenzie blushed. She grabbed her towel and dried her mouth. "No. Just happy I get to hang out with you next weekend. Mrs. White's a miracle worker."

"She's pretty awesome," Hannah said, rummaging through the bag for her toothbrush and paste. She uncapped the half-filled tube and squeezed a dollop of minty white goop onto her brush. "While I'm thinking about it, you should bring your dirty clothes. My mom won't care if you do a load. I always take mine home. It's way better than doing it at camp."

"Thanks." Makenzie beamed at Hannah's reflection in the

mirror. "It's a total pain washing clothes here. At least the sign-up sheet lets you know when it's your turn."

"It's still a hassle," Hannah said, sticking the brush in her mouth.

"See you tomorrow."

Mouth full of foam, Hannah nodded.

At Pinewood, Makenzie wriggled into her flannel pajamas and slipped into the comfort of her sleeping bag. Her body melted into the warm softness. It felt good to lie down. While she usually didn't mind, tonight she was thankful the cabin was quiet, minus six campers who talked after lights out and sometimes snored in their bunks.

She reached over and unzipped the small outside pocket of her backpack, fished out the ring, and slipped it on her finger. She'd started wearing the band at night since she couldn't during the day. After twisting it a few times around her finger, which had become an unexplainable habit, she flicked off the light switch.

Burrowed in the coziness of her down-filled bag, Makenzie's thoughts wandered to her parents. Pleased they agreed to let her stay at Hannah's, contentment washed over her like a soothing balm. *Maybe they aren't so overprotective after all.* With a smile, she drifted to sleep.

The girl ran the length of the expansive lawn to the dock. Arms bent stiffly at her side, hands grasping fistfuls of the long skirt's fabric. Where the wooden dock met the sand, she slowed, turning her head. Fearful eyes darted over her shoulder at the tall man who hurried down the Baldwin Manor stairs toward her. The girl's booted feet stepped quickly up the dock's few steps.

"Wait!" she cried out.

At the end of the dock, a man in a small boat pushed off the ladder with a paddle. The vessel drifted away from the wooden structure. At the sound of the girl's panicked voice, he turned. Without hesitation, he grabbed the second paddle, and in a few quick strokes, returned to the dock. He took hold of a ladder rung and hoisted himself up, not stopping to tether the boat.

Running down the dock, the girl looked behind her, catching a glimpse of the man hurrying toward her. Head turned, she didn't see the pile of rope, coiled like a snake, until her right foot stepped into it. Her left foot continued the pace, but she was caught. Hands clenched in the folds of her skirt, unable to catch her fall, the girl toppled like a fallen tree. Her head slammed into a thick metal cleat that jutted out of the dock with a dull thud. She lay motionless.

"Dakota!" the man running toward her screamed.

Makenzie woke, her body shaking uncontrollably. She sat up, taking deep breaths to calm her pounding heart. That odd dream again. But this time terrifying and realistic. *What did the man say?* She squinted in the dark, trying to pull the word from her subconscious.

Dakota? Was that the girl's name? Unanswered questions raced through her mind. She twisted the ring nervously while she tried falling back to sleep. At least her body tremors had stopped.

What's with these creepy dreams? Has the history of this place invaded my psyche? It was just a dream, not real. Not real. A mantra she told herself over and over, until she finally fell into a restless night's sleep.

Chapter Fifteen

Makenzie stood in front of the Zephyr Lodge, waving at the white minivan as it slowly climbed the winding drive out of camp. She exhaled when the vehicle turned out of sight, relieved the last of her campers was headed home. Another week of counsellor duties fulfilled, her attention shifted to the weekend ahead at Hannah's. Makenzie's stomach fluttered with anticipation as she walked to Pinewood, imagining how much fun they were going to have.

Focused on what she needed to pack, Makenzie didn't see Hannah waving at her from Silver Dollar's small porch. "Earth to Makenzie," Hannah hollered, walking off the wooden steps into her friend's line of vision.

"Oh, hey," Makenzie said, stopping. A wide grin replacing the faraway look on her face.

"Where the heck were you just now?"

"Thinking about the weekend." Makenzie's cheeks bloomed a rosy pink. "It's going to be super fun."

"It's awesome your parents finally said yes. My mom is picking us up in 30. Meet you in the parking lot, okay?"

"See you there."

At Pinewood, Makenzie threw enough clothes for two days in her backpack. Unzipping the pack's small outside pouch to grab the ring, her mind's eye flashed on the nightmare of the falling girl when her fingers wrapped around the cold metal. *That's odd. This morning was so busy, I'd forgotten last night's shocking dream.* Focused on meeting Hannah, Makenzie shook off the image of the girl and pushed the ring deep into the pocket of her jean shorts for safe keeping.

Remembering the invitation to do a load of laundry, Makenzie stuffed the pile of dirty clothes she'd shoved under the bed into her empty pillowcase. She sniffed the plaid flannel, wrinkling her nose. The makeshift laundry bag could use a wash as well.

Hannah and her mom were busy catching up when Makenzie approached the duo standing in front of the Bailey's SUV. It was obvious they were mother and daughter. Like Hannah, Mrs. Bailey was tall. Her strawberry blonde hair fell in soft waves around her shoulders. Two pair of similar green eyes greeted her when she stepped into their sight line.

"You must be Makenzie," Hannah's mom said, taking in her long black braids and blue eyes.

"I am. Thanks for the invite, Mrs. Bailey."

"We're delighted to have you. And please, call me Kelly," Hannah's mom said, taking the bulging pillow case from Makenzie and loading it into the SUV's rear compartment next to Hannah's gear. "Your backpack will fit in the back seat. Ready girls?"

On the way to the Bailey's home, Makenzie realized it was the first time she'd left camp in a month. Half of the summer had flown by. She winced. Each day brought her closer to returning to her overprotective parents. Not wanting to ruin the fun weekend ahead, she let the thought go and concentrated on the scenery. The SUV passed through neighbourhood streets lined with rustic homes shaded by tall pines, finally pulling into the driveway of a grey two-story house.

"Your dad and sister will be back from paddle boarding soon. Why don't you two get settled while I make some lunch."

"Thanks, Mom," Hannah said, opening the rear door of the SUV.

"Let me help carry some of this in the house. I'll put your pillowcase in the laundry room for later," Kelly said.

"That'd be great, thanks." Makenzie slung her backpack across her shoulders and followed Hannah up the flower-lined walkway and through the front door. She paused, taking in her first glimpse of the Bailey's home.

The living room echoed the natural beauty of the outdoors, giving off a warm, comforting vibe. Wood floors covered in neutral-coloured rugs paired with seasonal photos of the lake and surrounding mountains hung tastefully on the walls, made the space feel more like a cozy lodge. An over-sized couch draped with velvet textured throws sat vacant in front of a stone-lined fireplace. Makenzie imagined wrapping herself in one and cuddling up next to a roaring fire, sipping a mug of hot cocoa while snow dusted the pine trees outside the sliding glass door.

"My room is this way," Hannah said, leading Makenzie past a spacious kitchen and up a stairway to the second floor.

"So that's your dad and sister," Makenzie said, stopping to study the Bailey family portrait that greeted them at the top of the stairs. The denim clad family of four stood barefoot on the beach, wide smiles as bright as their white shirts, the lake like indigo stained glass behind them.

"Yeah. My mom had that taken before my sister, Kayla, went off to college. The family joked she might never come back. But she's way too much of a daddy's girl," Hannah said, continuing toward her room.

Makenzie stalled, admiring the pictures that lined the walls of the hallway. Kayla, a chubby-faced toddler, digging in the sand with a bright yellow shovel. Hannah, in a knit hat, building a snowman, her beaming smile minus a front tooth. The Baileys, wearing swimsuits, arms entwined around each other's waists, standing knee-deep in the lake, laughing as if the photographer had just said something funny. It was obvious how tight the family was, the images a pictorial history of their love of the outdoors and each other.

"Lunch is ready," Kelly called from downstairs.

"That was fast," Hannah said. The girls were sprawled out on Hannah's bed, discussing their weekend plans. "Coming, Mom."

"I hope you like taco salad," Kelly said. "It's Hannah's favourite. I always make it when she comes home for the weekend."

The island in the middle of the kitchen displayed numerous ingredients—from crunchy, bowl-shaped tortilla shells, to a variety of toppings.

"I do," Makenzie said, grabbing one of the plates containing an empty bowl waiting to be filled. Her stomach growled. "Guess I didn't know how hungry I was until now."

"Dig in, there's plenty. I made enough for a small army. Will and Kayla will be famished when they get back from paddle boarding."

Makenzie plopped a scoop of Spanish rice into the bottom of her bowl. Across from her, Kelly was busy making her salad. From their proximity, Makenzie noticed an iridescent white stone held captive by thin strands of silver entwined around it, dangling from a chain around her neck. Its simplicity was beautiful.

Hannah leaned forward to check it out.

"Really fabulous design, Mom. Is it for your jewelry store collection or did someone hire you to make it?"

"I'm working on matching earrings, then the trio will go to the jewellers."

"Mom's been making jewelry for years. She has quite a following with locals and tourists. Sometimes they'll order custom pieces. Which is cool."

"I'm fortunate to have a job I love. Thanks for the glowing advertisement," Kelly said, gazing affectionately at her daughter.

Makenzie's smile flattened. Momentarily envious of their close relationship, she tried to remember the last time a conversation with her own mom was lighthearted and loving. Their interactions these days were usually tense—her mom questioning her behaviour, asking if she was doing the right thing. She shook off the awkward feeling, then added a scoop of pinto beans on top of the rice.

The salad was delicious. And so was the banter that flowed around the table. Makenzie was privy to insights of Hannah's younger years from the funny stories Kelly shared.

"And then she toddled over to the robotic dinosaur which was as tall as she was, picked it up, and said, 'It's no scary.'"

Makenzie laughed, causing the last gooey bite on her fork to slide off and land in her lap. She looked down at the avocado smeared mess on her shorts. Wiping it up with her napkin made it worse. "Thanks for lunch, which I'm now wearing."

"The washing machine is available if you want to do your laundry now," Kelly said. "Hannah can show you where it is."

"That'd be great. I'll run up and change so I can throw these in too. Be right back."

Digging through her backpack for a clean pair of shorts, Makenzie heard voices from downstairs trickle into the bedroom. Hannah's dad and sister were back. Anxious to meet them, she changed quickly and hurried downstairs carrying her dirty shorts, forgetting about the ring buried in the front pocket.

Chapter Sixteen

"**W**hat's that heavenly smell?" Makenzie was nestled in the warm covers of one of the twin beds in Hannah's room, eyes closed, nose fully awake.

"Waffles. It's a Bailey family weekend tradition," Hannah answered, her voice groggy.

"Yum," Makenzie said, with a yawn. The girls had stayed up late the night before watching *Princess Bride,* one of Hannah's favourite movies.

As if on cue, Kelly's voice floated up the stairs. "Morning, sleepy heads. Breakfast is ready."

The kitchen table resembled a page from a culinary magazine. Plates of steaming waffles accompanied by crispy bacon and glasses of bright orange juice invited the girls to take a seat. A rainbow of sliced fruit in clear glass bowls and a miniature pitcher of syrup waited for them to top their waffles.

"This looks amazing," Makenzie said, reaching for the bowl of blueberries.

"As always, Mom. Where's Dad and Kayla?"

"Your dad is on a bike ride and Kayla just left for work at the marina."

"They're missing out," Hannah said, drenching the golden squares topped with a mound of strawberries in syrup.

"Nope. Kayla ate, and I'll keep some warm in the oven for your dad."

Makenzie's taste buds did a happy dance while she chewed the first bite. "It's delicious, thank you."

"Glad you like it. By the way, is this yours?" Kelly fished into the front pocket of her Lake Tahoe sweatshirt, her hand making a lump in the fabric. She withdrew her clenched fingers and placed a small object on the table in front of the girls. In the mere seconds it took to register what it was, Makenzie's ring changed the previously chill energy that swirled around them.

"I found it in the dryer."

Makenzie watched as Hannah's eyes, playful the moment before, turned an icy gaze her way.

"Y-y-yes, it is," Makenzie stammered. The colour drained from her face. "I found it in the lake."

She dropped her chin to her chest. The bite of waffle did

somersaults in her stomach, threatening to come back up. Makenzie gulped, willing it to stay down, sure the shame she felt at being caught in her lie stained her cheeks cherry red.

"Well, it's very unusual. The stone is an alexandrite, which is somewhat rare. It's made of the mineral chrysoberyl, which enables it to change colour," Kelly said, oblivious to her daughter's sudden, quiet anger and Makenzie's obvious embarrassment.

Out of the corner of her eye, Makenzie stole a glance at Hannah. Silent, she had continued eating.

"I've noticed the colour change. And sometimes the skin under the ring feels warm and tingles. Is that normal?" Makenzie asked tentatively.

"Hmm, I've not heard that," Kelly said. She picked the band up again, then turned it over to examine the setting underneath the heart-shaped stone. "There's a small space between the stone and the wearer's skin. If the stone was set so it lay flat that might explain it, but I've never heard of alexandrite having that effect."

"It only happened a few times. Maybe it was just my imagination."

"The setting appears to be older. Possibly from the 1960s," Kelly said, studying the stone once more before returning it to the table.

"If it's that old, it could have been lost decades ago," Makenzie said, in an attempt to get Hannah to hear one of the reasons she'd rationalized it was okay to keep it.

"Maybe," Kelly said, picking up the empty blueberry bowl and returning to the kitchen.

Makenzie watched Hannah eat the last bite on her plate. She gulped her juice and stood, grabbed her dirty dishes, and put them in the sink, ignoring Makenzie.

"Thanks for breakfast, Mom," Hannah said on her way out of the kitchen. She stomped up the stairs with heavy footsteps.

Makenzie slumped in her chair. The previously crisp waffles were ruined, soggy in a puddle of syrup and blueberries. She couldn't eat them anyway. Her stomach felt like it was tied in knots. She'd d been so careful hiding the ring. The fun she was having at Hannah's made her slip up. Was keeping the band worth losing a friend? It had been so easy to come up with reasons why it was okay for her not to turn the ring in. *My parents are right not to trust me. I don't always do the honourable thing.*

Makenzie knocked softly on the closed bedroom door. Silence. After a few moments, the knob twisted and the door swung open. Hannah walked over to her bed, sat, and stared down at her phone, ignoring Makenzie. Taking in a deep breath to bolster her courage, she entered the room and sat on the bed across from Hannah.

"I'm really sorry I lied about the ring," Makenzie said softly.

Hannah tossed her phone on the bed and looked out the bedroom window.

"I was going to turn it in, but for some reason, I just couldn't.

Because it was lost, I told myself the owner probably didn't expect to find it. So why not keep it? I started wearing the band at night, then I'd take it off in the morning. The stone changed colours, which I thought was unusual. And like I told your mom, sometimes the skin underneath the stone would tingle and feel warm."

Hannah turned her head toward Makenzie, but kept her eyes down, focused on the phone that lay by her side.

Encouraged, Makenzie continued. "A few times when I fell asleep with it on, I had strange dreams about a girl in historic clothing. At first, she was on the boat dock in front of the Baldwin Manor meeting a guy in a paddle boat. Then she was scared, running away from a man who came out of the manor."

Still nothing.

"In my last dream, the girl fell on the dock, hitting her head with a thud on one of those metal cleats boats get tied up to. She didn't move. It was so realistic. I woke up trembling."

Hannah lifted her head. Her cool stare met Makenzie's blue eyes.

Finally, Makenzie verbalized her suspicions. "I can't explain it, but I feel like the ring is trying to tell me something."

She knew it sounded crazy. Even she thought it was. Her admission hung in the air like a storm cloud between them in the awkward silence that followed.

"That's interesting," Hannah snapped, "but you heard my mom. The stone can change colours, so that's not unusual. I don't know what those weird dreams mean, but it doesn't sound like they have anything to do with the ring. You're just telling yourself that so you'll feel better about keeping it, which isn't right," Hannah said. The tone of her voice mirrored her icy gaze.

Makenzie looked away, absorbing her friend's biting words. The ring being tied to her dreams made sense at camp. Now she wasn't so sure, it did sound far-fetched. Maybe Hannah was right. She was telling herself they were linked so she'd feel better about not doing the right thing.

But would she still have had those odd dreams if she'd turned in the band the day she found it? There was only one way to reclaim her friendship with Hannah.

"I'll turn the ring in when we get back to camp," Makenzie said, looking directly at Hannah. She watched the frost in her friend's eyes melt a little. "You can go with me to see Mrs. White so you'll know I've kept my word this time," she added.

As Hannah nodded her head, the corners of her mouth turned up into a small smile.

Chapter Seventeen

"Thanks for the fun weekend," Makenzie said to Hannah's mom. The girls' gear, lumped in a pile behind the Bailey's SUV, waited to be carried to their respective cabins.

"It was my pleasure. Let me help you two with your bags."

"No, we're good," Hannah answered. "We need to stop by Mrs. White's office first." She shot a piercing glance at Makenzie whose cheeks turned rosy underneath her sun-kissed cheeks.

"Have a great week. Hannah, I'll pick you up on Friday. Makenzie, I hope you enjoy the rest of the summer at Camp Baldwin."

"Thanks, Kelly," Makenzie said, bending over to pick up her backpack and freshly laundered pillowcase stuffed with clean, folded clothes. "I will."

But now that they were at camp, butterflies flitted around her stomach at the thought of turning in the ring.

"See you soon, Mom," Hannah said. She hoisted her duffel bag over her shoulder and followed Makenzie to the camp director's office.

Through the mesh of the closed screen door, Mrs. White sat at her desk reading, glasses perched at the end of her nose. The girls unloaded their gear on the chairs that sat on the front porch. Makenzie crossed the index and middle fingers of her left hand and hoped for the best, while her right hand knocked on the screen door's metal frame.

Mrs. White looked up from her paperwork. "Come in, girls. How was your weekend away?"

Makenzie stepped into the office, butterflies no longer flitting, they swirled inside her belly. Her throat was dry. Hannah, who trailed behind Makenzie, looked at her expectantly.

"I-i-it was nice," Makenzie said, trying to find her voice. "Umm," she fished into the front pocket of her shorts and retrieved the ring. "I found this in the lake. One of the camp rules is to turn items in to lost and found, so I'm turning it in," Makenzie said, words pouring out of her mouth in a rush. Cheeks burning, she approached the desk and set the ring on an uncluttered patch of wood in front of a somewhat confused Mrs. White, who looked down at the band.

It took a moment for Makenzie's words to sink in and for the camp director to realize what had been found. She picked up the ring to examine it.

"This is quite a find," Mrs. White said. She looked up from the band to meet Makenzie's eyes. "Where exactly in the lake were you?"

"Sitting on the camp dock. The ring was underwater, wedged between some rocks. I dove in and picked it up." With each word, the butterflies in her stomach flitted slowly away, leaving an empty, hollow feeling in her gut.

"No one has inquired about a lost ring. I'm not a jeweller, but it looks old and possibly expensive."

Quiet until now, Hannah chimed in. "My mom told us the stone is an alexandrite, which is rare and pricey. She said the stone is made up of some mineral that makes it change colour."

"I've noticed it a few times," Makenzie added.

"That's right, Hannah," Mrs. White said, eyeing the ring. "Kelly makes jewelry. Of course, she would know. When did you find it?" She looked up at Makenzie.

"Right before camp started," Makenzie admitted, head down, her eyes unable to meet the director's inquisitive gaze.

"Oh, I see," Mrs. White said. An uncomfortable silence filled the office. "Normally, the camp rule for lost and found is that if something isn't claimed in a week, the person who found the item gets to keep it."

A flicker of hope lit in the pit of Makenzie's stomach.

"However," Mrs. White added, "due to the ring being a valuable and unusual find, if its owner comes forward in the future, it's only fair, Makenzie, that I contact you so it can be returned."

"O-o-of course," Makenzie sputtered.

"Thank you for turning in the ring. You did the right thing."

"Finally," Hannah whispered soft enough for only Makenzie to hear. She watched Hannah's eyes narrow at Mrs. White's comment. Relief washed over her when Hannah didn't mention Makenzie's carelessness had caught her in a lie.

"Thanks," Makenzie said weakly.

"I'll mention the lost ring to the counsellors during lunch announcements today before camp starts," Mrs. White said. "And since you found it weeks ago, I'll also email the parents of campers who've attended camp in the past, letting them know about the recovered ring."

"Hopefully whoever it belongs to will come forward," Makenzie said. She tried to sound convincing. But in her heart, she hoped no one would.

Mrs. White opened her top desk drawer, set the band in the corner, and closed it.

"Since you're here, you should know we're starting to prepare in earnest for the Baldwin Manor's 100th Anniversary Celebration at the end of the summer. While it won't affect camper schedules, counsellor schedules will change when it's your turn to help out."

The girls nodded in unison. Makenzie exhaled, grateful the

conversation was no longer focused on the ring. In the distance, the clang of the triangle signalled lunch time.

"See you at the Chuck House," Mrs. White said.

Wrapped in the warmth of her sleeping bag, Makenzie listened to the quiet breathing of Pinewood's sleeping campers. In the darkness, her left hand reached for the band on her bare right ring finger. The comforting habit of twisting the ring before she fell asleep was gone. *When would her subconscious get a clue and stop?*

Makenzie sighed, thinking about Hannah and their return to camp. She'd been nice enough after they'd met with Mrs. White. But something had definitely changed. While friendly, Hannah was distant—not seeking Makenzie out to sit with her at lunch or dinner like she had before.

What did I expect? I lied about turning in the ring and got caught. Would I want to be friends with someone like that? My parents were right. I still need their constant supervision. Turning 13 wasn't a magic switch that meant you were grown up all of a sudden. If only I had listened to Hannah in the first place.

Finally, the negative thoughts swirling in her head faded and Makenzie fell asleep.

Chapter Eighteen

"Hi, Thomas. We're here to help hang lights for the 100th Anniversary Celebration," Makenzie said. She and Naomi approached the caretaker who was bent over, rummaging through a large crate full of clear light strings. Each lump of miniature bulbs, affixed to dark green cords, was a tangled mess.

"I don't know who put these away last year," Thomas said, frowning. "They're a disaster." His brown eyes looked up at the girls with frustration, then back down at the lights. He let out an audible sigh, scratched his head, and folded his arms across his chest.

The trio stood in the Baldwin Manor garden where the Roaring 20s dance party would take place at the end of camp. Mrs. White had excused the girls from afternoon beach duty so they could help.

Apparently, the project would take several afternoons.

Wanting to be helpful, Makenzie reached into the crate and pulled out a ball of lights. She turned it over, searching for the end with the plug. When she founded it, she began weaving the plastic square through the spaghetti-like lump. As she worked, she gently shook the jumbled strand to loosen the maze, encouraging the knotted heap to come undone easier. After several minutes, Makenzie laid the result of her efforts, an untangled six-foot strand, out on the garden's lush lawn.

"It's not as bad as you think." She looked up at Thomas with a grin.

He nodded approvingly, but didn't offer up a smile. "Nice work. I need to take care of something. Why don't you two work on this mess for a bit. I'll hang the untangled strands when I get back."

"Sure thing," Naomi said, grabbing a cluster of lights.

The girls watched Thomas' back as he ambled away toward his office.

"He doesn't seem very happy," Naomi remarked. She sat down on the lawn, searched for the end with the square electric prong, and began working it loose from the tangle.

"No, he's not. I think he's lonely." Makenzie plopped down on the grass with another jumbled light set.

"Why do you think that?"

"His eyes are sad, and he's always alone." Makenzie reasoned. "I rarely see him talking to anyone, and he never smiles."

"You seem to know a lot about him," Naomi said, the strand of lights grew longer as she worked.

"Not really. I've taken the tour he gives Baldwin campers a few times. He knows a lot about the manor and Lake Tahoe. He reminds me of my grandpa, only way less happy and funny."

"That's more intel than I have." Finished with her first strand, Naomi laid it out next to the one Makenzie had untangled and grabbed another.

Makenzie paused, wondering if she should confide in Naomi.

"Sometimes, to see if I can accomplish them, I give myself little challenges. When I met Thomas, it bothered me that he seemed so unhappy. So, I challenged myself to make him smile." Not sure how Naomi would react to her silly game, Makenzie was thankful her eyes were focused on the light strand splayed across her lap so she couldn't see her reaction.

"That's interesting. Too bad untangling that first string of lights didn't get you a smile."

"I know," Makenzie said, relieved Naomi didn't think she was odd.

"It's going to be harder than I thought. At least I've got a few more weeks until camp ends."

The girls sat in the shade of a towering pine, untangling the lights in compatible silence. Their focus on undoing the maze of strings became a hypnotic task, each strand a unique ball of knots to unwind.

Even though she'd told herself not to, Makenzie couldn't stop thinking about the ring. She couldn't explain why she was drawn to it, she just wished she'd get the band back. Looking down at her bare finger only intensified her feelings. Mrs. White had put a note on the camp bulletin board: *Lost ring found. See Mrs. White to claim.* It was only Tuesday. Five more days of waiting.

When Thomas returned, almost half of the crate's light strings were laid out on the lawn, ready to be hung.

"Thanks for the help," Thomas said gruffly, his somber demeanour unchanged, but Makenzie noticed the hardness in his eyes soften when he looked down at the snake-like strands.

"I'll take it from here. Mrs. White wants you to return to camp."

"I'm open," a tall camper shouted, waving her arms above her head. The girl with the basketball grasped tightly at her chest thrust the ball at the tall girl. She dribbled, then shot from her vantage point near the basket, scoring two points. Cheers erupted from sideline spectators.

Campers were leisurely scattered around Zephyr Lodge and the blacktop, enjoying their hour of free time before dinner, when Makenzie and Naomi returned from helping Thomas.

At the opposite end of the blacktop, Hannah and one of her cabinmates were competing in an aggressive game of ping-pong. Makenzie joined the crowd circled around the table so she could cheer Hannah on.

"What's the score?" Makenzie asked one of the onlookers.

"Maddie is up by two. If she gets this point, she wins."

"You got this, Hannah!" Makenzie hollered.

Recognizing Makenzie's voice, Hannah turned. She nodded, but didn't smile.

Maddie served and the girls volleyed back and forth competitively several times until Hannah missed a quick cross-table shot, making Maddie the winner.

"I'm up next," said a boy in a sky-blue Camp Baldwin shirt. He walked over and took the wooden paddle from Hannah.

"I hope you have better luck than I did," she said with a smile, then turned to leave.

"Hannah, wait up," Makenzie said, jogging toward her.

Hannah stopped and turned.

"What's up?" Her smile deflated as she looked at Makenzie.

Makenzie was taken aback by the coolness in her voice. "Um, just wondering how your week is going. We haven't talked much."

Unfeeling green eyes studied Makenzie for a few seconds. "It's going fine. Anything else?" Hannah said abruptly. Her freckled nose tilted upward with an air of defiance.

Makenzie's heart sank. *She's still angry. Even though I kept my word and turned in the ring*—the very thing she thought would allow her to make peace with Hannah and preserve their newfound friendship. She was wrong. Sadness crept in her chest, thick like honey. It flowed onto her shoulders, making them slump.

"No," Makenzie said weakly. *I miss hanging out with you*, she wanted to add, but didn't.

"Well then, I'll see you around," Hannah said. She turned and walked away.

Chapter Nineteen

akenzie waved goodbye to her last camper, the girl's profile barely visible in the back of her family's mini-van as it crawled up the winding drive.

At the edge of the parking lot, Makenzie noticed Hannah and her mom loading their SUV. When her gaze met Makenzie's, Kelly smiled and waved. Hannah looked toward Makenzie with a blank stare, ignoring her, then turned away. She opened the passenger door and disappeared behind the window's tinted glass when the door slammed shut.

Makenzie returned Kelly's wave, then dropped her hand with a sigh. Her feelings were as tangled as the light strands she'd helped unravel. While she was relieved Hannah and her animosity toward her were leaving for a couple of days, her heart was clouded with sadness. It wasn't the same without Hannah's companionship. With only two weeks until the 100th Anniversary Celebration and the end of camp, Makenzie had hoped Hannah would forgive her so they could enjoy what little time was left as friends.

"Makenzie, can I see you in my office?" Mrs. White said, startling her.

"Of course." She trailed behind the camp director, her mind a whirl. *Had she done something wrong?* Her previous angst about Hannah redirected to why she was being summoned.

The office screen door let out a whiny creak as it closed. Makenzie followed Mrs. White to her desk and waited in confused anticipation.

"It hasn't been a full week yet, so if someone comes forward, I'll know where to find it," Mrs. White explained. She smiled, calming the butterflies that flitted in Makenzie's stomach, then opened her desk drawer and retrieved the ring from the corner where she'd placed it days before. She paused momentarily, studying the heart-shaped stone, then placed the band on the edge of her desk.

An exhalation of relief mixed with surprise rushed from Makenzie's chest. She hadn't realized she'd been holding her breath until it escaped.

"Really? Wow!" A smile illuminated her face. She picked up the band and slipped it on her finger. The butterflies from minutes before were quelled by a warm happiness that flowed in her belly. She looked up at Mrs. White. "Thank you."

"You're most welcome. Now back to camp business. With the 100th Anniversary Celebration swiftly approaching, I've offered Thomas the assistance of Camp Baldwin's counsellors this weekend. He's behind in many tasks that need to be completed for the Roaring 20s Dance Party."

Makenzie nodded in agreement. It took effort for her to look at Mrs. White and not the ring. She hoped she appeared to be listening intently on the outside because her insides were in the middle of a happy dance.

"After lunch, you and Naomi will help Thomas finish the light string project in the Baldwin Manor garden," Mrs. White instructed.

"Of course," Makenzie answered. Reunited with the ring and given a task for the weekend, she'd forgotten Hannah's anger.

"Great. There'll be another assignment once the garden project is completed. I appreciate your help."

"No problem," Makenzie said, turning to leave. She looked down at the stone on her finger; it was the bright blue of a cloudless day. Her heart soared. Sometimes wishes do come true.

The half-filled crate of tangled lights waited for Makenzie and Naomi on the emerald garden lawn. The girls waved their hellos to Thomas, who was perched on a ladder in the far corner of the garden, weaving strings of lights in the branches of a massive pine. He responded with a curt nod. After grabbing handfuls of strands, the girls sat on the grass and began untangling the cords.

"The 100th Anniversary Celebration is going to be a blast," Naomi said, looking down. She studied the knotted green cord in her lap, while her hands worked the strand back to a straight line.

"I know." Makenzie mimicked Naomi's actions with the light string bunched in her hands, fingers adeptly loosening the jumbled cord as she worked, making it easier to untangle. "What'd you bring to wear?"

"My mom went to a costume party as a flapper girl one year. She let me borrow her sleeveless, gold-beaded dress and a long fake pearl necklace to help make it look more authentic."

"Nice," Makenzie said. As her hands worked the light strings, she caught glimpses of the ring when her right hand darted out from under the knotted cord. In the afternoon light, the stone was a calming shade of turquoise, mimicking Makenzie's mood. Thrilled the band had been returned, her initial excitement had morphed into contentment.

"What about you?" Naomi asked. Finished with a strand, she stood and laid it out on the lawn next to the crate and grabbed another.

"My mom took me to a thrift store. We found a vintage, pink velvet, drop-waisted dress trimmed with gold lace. The shop had some ivory, satin opera gloves that go up my arms, just over my elbows. We added a hot pink feathered boa to complete the outfit."

"Sounds like a fun outing, and a really cool costume," Naomi said.

"You know, it *was* fun," Makenzie said wistfully, remembering the day. Her mom had suggested it, uncharacteristically. They'd cracked up when her mom tried on silly hats, taking on a new persona for each one. And they went to lunch at Makenzie's favourite restaurant. That day, her mom wasn't on her to do the right thing or constantly reminding her about homework or swim practice. She smiled at the memory.

"Bring some light strands over," Thomas hollered from across the garden, pulling Makenzie out of her reverie.

"Will do," Makenzie shouted back. She'd just finished unwinding the strand on her lap.

She got up and went to the pile of untangled cords resting by the crate. Bending over, Makenzie scooped up several strands like a load of firewood, hugging them to her chest as she stood. She walked slowly over to Thomas, the ends of the cords hanging down on either side danced lightly on the ground.

"Here you go," Makenzie said, laying the strands down gently at the base of the ladder.

"Hand one up," Thomas said.

Makenzie grabbed one of the cords and extended it in her clenched right fist toward Thomas who bent over the ladder to retrieve it. His outstretched hand stopped in midair when he looked down. His eyes opened wide in surprise, then narrowed. Friendly a second before, Makenzie watched his warm gaze turn cold.

"Where'd you find that?" Thomas snapped, his voice a low growl between clenched teeth. He stared at the string of lights in her hand.

Makenzie stepped back, confused by the sudden change in his demeanour.

"The lights?" She looked down at her shaking hand and glimpsed the ring. The stone's previous turquoise shade had changed to a dark sapphire.

"No. The ring," Thomas growled, stepping down off the ladder.

"In the l-l-ake," Makenzie sputtered, taken completely off guard. She let go of the strand and felt it drop at her feet. Thomas' eyes bored into the band. She moved her hand behind her, hiding it from view while her mind raced.

Her fragmented thoughts flashed to the day Thomas stood at the end of the Baldwin Manor boat dock, peering down at the lake. *What had he said?*

Makenzie's brow furrowed as she struggled to recall. The words came to her, as if he'd whispered them in her ear.

"I lost something here a long time ago. Something I'll never get back."
Could it be?

"Is this what you lost?" Makenzie revealed her hand from behind her back and held it out. Her fingers trembled.

"It is."

Thomas lunged forward, reaching toward Makenzie's hand. His fingertips brushed hers as she recoiled in shock, turned, and fled. Her pounding heart ached as she ran. If it wasn't caged in her chest, she felt it would take flight.

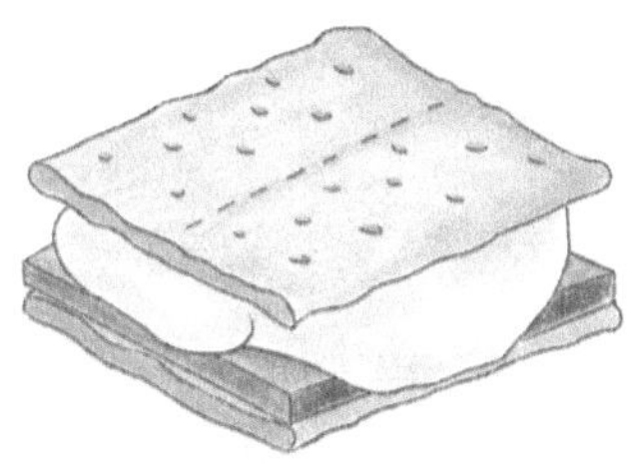

Chapter Twenty

akenzie's feet flew up the worn, wooden steps to Pinewood's small porch. She flung the cabin door open and slammed it shut behind her. Fingers shaking, she turned the metal deadbolt to the right, locking the door. The breath she'd been holding escaped in a rush. Relieved to be ensconced in the safety of the cabin, Makenzie flopped down on the bed. Her body lay still while her thoughts raced.

The ring belonged to Thomas. But how? Makenzie raised her hand over her eyes to study the band. *What secrets did the silent stone hold?* She desperately wished Hannah hadn't gone home so she'd have someone to talk to about Thomas' shocking reaction. But given Hannah's unfriendliness toward her, Makenzie doubted she'd even care.

But Jessica would. Makenzie got up, swiped her phone off the rickety nightstand, and slipped it in her back pocket. She inhaled, gathering her courage, before unlocking the cabin door. She opened it slowly, just enough to peer out at the vacant dirt swath in the middle of Cabin Row.

In a flash, Makenzie was out the door, down the steps, and on the trail that led to the Baldwin Manor boat dock. Her heart raced as she ran down the tree-lined path, thankful she was somewhat hidden. The trees thinned out as she approached the boathouse and nearby dock.

Tourists milled around the grounds taking pictures. Some stopped to read the placards placed around the historic property. Cody, dressed in her vintage navy outfit, sat in front of the boathouse gazing out toward the water. She looked up at Makenzie and waved.

While her hand reached up to return Cody's greeting, Makenzie scanned the area for Thomas. Grateful there was no sign of him, she jogged to the end of dock and retrieved her phone from her back pocket. She sat facing the Baldwin Manor in case Thomas came into view.

"Hi, Jess," Makenzie's dry mouth cracked into the phone. "How are you?"

"Hey, stranger. I'm fine. Haven't heard from you in a while. I suppose you've been too busy at camp to call?" Makenzie heard the initial surprise in Jessica's voice turn to irritation.

"I know," Makenzie said lamely, adding guilt to the swirl of emotions churning in her chest. "We've been getting ready for the 100th Anniversary Celebration," she offered as an excuse.

"Oh, I forgot about that. How's it going?" Jessica asked politely, but she didn't really sound interested.

"It was fine until a bit ago," Makenzie said. She gulped and continued. "Remember the ring I found?"

"Yeah. What about it?"

"It's kind of a long story," Makenzie said. Her worried eyes scanned the milling crowd of tourists.

"I've got time."

Makenzie took in a deep breath, then exhaled. "Hannah invited me to stay the weekend and her mom found it in the washing machine."

"So now you're hanging out at her house?" Jessica said in a huff. Her voice dripped with jealously. "Why is her mom finding the ring a problem?"

Makenzie hesitated. It was time to fess up. Her cheeks burned.

"Because I lied to her," the words tumbled out.

"I'm confused, Kenzie. Why did you lie?" Jessica asked.

"The camp rule is if you find something, you have to turn it in. If the owner doesn't claim it in a week, it's yours. I never turned it in."

"Okay, now I get it. But why didn't you?"

"It's hard to explain," Makenzie said, her gaze still on the lookout. "I was going to, but something happened when I looked at the stone. I felt compelled to keep it. Because I found the ring in the lake, I didn't think anyone would claim it. So I kept it hidden in my pocket or in my backpack. Sometimes at night I'd put it on before I fell asleep."

"That's kinda weird," Jessica muttered.

Unsettled, Makenzie squirmed on the dock. No sign of Thomas. Her eyes, focused on the distant crowd, relaxed.

"And then, when Hannah's mom returned the ring, Hannah got really angry. She's a real stickler about camp rules."

"So sorry your new friend got mad," Jessica snickered. "What does that have to do with what's going on now?"

"I said it was a long story," Makenzie said calmly. She hoped her demeanour would rub off on Jess. "We turned the ring in when we got back to camp. The director said if it wasn't claimed, I could keep it."

"So, did turning it in help? Is Hannah still upset with you?"

"Hmmm," Makenzie chewed on her lower lip. "Not as much as I thought it would. She's not mad, but she isn't as friendly either."

"Bummer," Jessica said cheerfully.

Makenzie ignored her friend's jab and continued.

"The camp director gave me back the ring earlier today." Makenzie looked down at her hand and studied the stone. Its current shade mirrored the aquamarine water that lapped against the dock pilings.

"That's what you wanted, isn't it? So what's the problem?"

Makenzie could tell by the irritation in Jessica's voice she was losing her patience.

"Yeah. But then I was helping Thomas, the Baldwin Manor caretaker, hang some lights for the 100th Anniversary Celebration, and he saw the ring. He's usually pretty standoffish, but he got super angry."

"I'm not following you. Why would he do that?"

"He said the ring is his." The words tumbled out of Makenzie's mouth in a rush. "And then he tried to grab my hand, but I ran."

"What?! That's crazy! Are you okay?"

Stinging tears welled in Makenzie's eyes. A wave of relief washed over her, catching her off guard. Her best friend's concern comforted her like a warm blanket.

"Yeah. But the crazier thing is, I think he's right."

"How could the ring belong to him?" Jessica asked.

"When camp first started, I saw him at the beach in front of the Baldwin Manor staring out at the lake. He looked really sad. When I asked him about it, he said he'd lost something there a long time ago. Something he'd never get back."

"Whoa. You can't assume he meant the ring."

"But what else could it be? He just told me the ring is his." Frustrated, Makenzie's angst flew out of her mouth. "I should have listened to Hannah, turned the ring in, and forgot about it."

"Sounds like Hannah knows best. Why'd you even bother calling me? Why don't you just talk to her?" Jessica ranted into the phone.

"She's not here," Makenzie said through clenched teeth. "I wanted to talk to you. Look, I'm super sorry you broke your leg and had to miss camp. But you can't expect me not to make friends while I'm here. You'll always be my best friend. No one can change that."

"It sure doesn't feel like it. You promised to keep in touch and you haven't. And when you do, it's because Hannah is mad. That's not how you treat a best friend. Do your parents know about the ring?" Makenzie could almost taste the bitterness in Jessica's words.

"No," Makenzie answered meekly. Her aching chest slumped inward.

"Maybe you should tell them," Jessica hissed and hung up.

Chapter Twenty-One

It was no use trying to sleep. Makenzie couldn't pry her thoughts off the emotional roller coaster they were riding. She lay in the dark quiet of Pinewood, grateful the door had a lock and that Naomi was just a few feet away in the cabin next door. After her awful conversation with Jessica, she'd found Naomi and stuck close to her for the rest of the day, relieved Thomas hadn't come looking for her at camp.

Makenzie couldn't shake the sting of Jess's words. *"Do your parents know about the ring?"* They were a verbal punch in the gut. She should have told them. Or done the right thing and turned the band in the day she'd found it. But she hadn't and here she was.

Throughout their years as best friends, Jessica had never been this mad. *What if I've ruined our friendship forever?* Her heart ached deep in her chest. She could handle Hannah ignoring her for the short remainder of camp, but not losing Jess.

Her parents were right to be overprotective. She didn't always live up to their expectations. Their disappointment whispered in her ear. *"You knew the rules but didn't obey them. How can we trust you to be on your own if you don't do the right thing?"* Just thinking about how they'd react when they found out made her cheeks burn. Unconsciously, her left thumb and middle finger twisted the band around the ring finger of her right hand.

Stop feeling sorry for yourself and find a way to fix this. She brushed away the tears that stung her eyes with the back of her hand. The excitement she'd felt when she'd found the ring had vanished. To keep it, she had lied not only to Hannah, but to herself. *What made me think I'd get away with it? Just because I found the ring didn't make it mine.*

After trying so hard to keep the ring, she didn't want it anymore. She slipped the band off and set it with a thunk on the edge of the nightstand. Taking it off made the heavy weight in her chest feel a bit lighter.

Ideas bounced around her head like the silver metal ball in a pinball machine. Maybe she could fix this without her parents knowing. Wasn't that what they wanted in the long run? Actually, they wanted a daughter who didn't get into a mess like this, but if she did, wouldn't they be proud of her if she ultimately did the right thing? Makenzie chewed on her bottom lip, forming a plan. It was simple really. Tomorrow, she'd find Thomas and give him the ring.

Chapter Twenty-Two

Burrowed in the warmth of her sleeping bag, Makenzie lingered in the safe halo of sleep as long as she could. In the distance, the Chuck House triangle rang, waking her. Thoughts from the day before invaded her consciousness, carving a hollow feeling in her chest. The excitement of Mrs. White returning the ring, followed by Thomas' unexpected revelation that it belonged to him, ending with Jessica's anger toward her was a triple whammy. All in one day.

Makenzie took in a deep breath and opened her eyes. The ring, resting on the corner of the nightstand, sparkled, its stone the brilliant blue of a morning summer sky.

Why did I get so caught up in it? she wondered as the breath escaped from her mouth. *What am I going to do now?*

It belongs to Thomas. She should just return it, like she had decided the night before. But he was so angry, and confiding in Jessica had backfired.

"Do your parents know?" Jess's words were a fresh sting when she replayed the tape. Her parents. They were the only two left she could talk to about this mess. Hannah would return to camp in a few hours, but she'd made it clear she didn't want anything to do with her.

Makenzie could give the ring back to Mrs. White, tell her what happened with Thomas, she reasoned. But at some point, the camp director would call her parents. It would be better if they heard the story from her. The thought of their disappointment slowly crept into her chest, making it feel heavy.

Makenzie's stomach growled, protesting that she'd slept in and wasn't at the Chuck House eating breakfast. She sat up and reached for the Camp Baldwin sweatshirt at the foot of her sleeping bag to ward off the morning chill. She'd call her parents after she ate. Not only would the diversion appease her empty belly, it would also give her time to work up some courage. It was Saturday, after all. Their weekly check-in day. Disenchanted with the ring and the bad luck it had brought her, Makenzie plucked the band off the nightstand and dropped it into the small, front pocket of her backpack.

Headed to the Baldwin Manor dock to call her parents, Makenzie was at a complete loss about what to say. The French toast in her stomach, delicious minutes before, was doing cartwheels.

"Hi, Mom. I lied about turning in a ring I found and now Jessica and Hannah are really mad and the man who says it's his tried to grab it from me."

A mischievous grin tugged at the corners of her mouth. That would catch her mom by surprise. The momentary smile faded. This was serious. She needed to present the truth in a way her parents would understand, and hopefully, they'd be on her side about the whole messy thing.

Preoccupied, Makenzie didn't see Cody standing in front of the boathouse until she nearly walked into her.

"Hi. I haven't talked to you lately," Cody said. "Are you heading for your morning swim?"

Caught off guard, Makenzie stopped abruptly, taking in Cody's vintage, navy dress and the boathouse pamphlet sticking out of her pocket. Happy to see her friend, the worried look on her face melted away. Running into Cody was a welcome distraction from the call she wasn't prepared to make.

"Oh, hey, it has been a while." Makenzie gave Cody a small awkward wave. "Actually, I'm skipping practice to call my parents." She looked down and studied the flip-flops on her trail-dusted feet. The turmoil she felt about the difficult conversation she was about to have made her unsure of herself. When she raised her head,

Cody was eyeing her intently.

"Do you miss them?" Cody asked. "You seem a little sad."

Makenzie exhaled, unaware she'd been holding her breath. "Not sad, really. Nervous is more like it. It won't be an easy conversation." Makenzie didn't know why she was being so honest. She liked Cody, but barely knew her.

"Why is that?"

Makenzie hesitated, thinking about how much to say. Figuring she had nothing to lose, she dove in. "It's a bit of a long story."

Cody smiled. "I've got time. Or at least until someone wants to know about the Baldwin family boathouse."

Still early in the morning, only a few tourists milled around, hugging coffee cups purchased at the bakery truck that frequented the parking lot, while they gleaned information about the historic property from plaques posted at each structure.

"It started when I found a ring in the lake."

"Oh, you found it," Cody said excitedly.

Startled by her reaction, Makenzie searched Cody's face. It almost sounded like she knew what Makenzie was talking about.

"I mean, how wonderful, to find a ring." The enthusiasm in Cody's voice lessened, but her eyes sparkled. "I'm curious, what does it look like?"

"It's a gold band with a heart-shaped stone that often changes from pale blue to a deep sapphire. I'm told it's an alexandrite," Makenzie said. She watched the shine in Cody's eyes dwindle as her gaze shifted toward the Baldwin Manor. They brightened again when she looked back at Makenzie.

"It sounds beautiful," Cody said softly.

"It is. I should've turned the ring in to the camp's lost and found, but I didn't," Makenzie confessed. "It's strange really, and hard to explain. I felt compelled to keep it. And because I found the band in the lake, I told myself it had probably been lost for a long time so the owner wouldn't be able to claim it."

Cody gave an understanding nod. "That's reasonable. Go on."

Encouraged, Makenzie told Cody everything, starting with how she kept the ring hidden from Hannah, to Thomas saying it was his. She ended with her conversation with Jessica, resulting in the decision to call her parents. Even though she knew they would be disappointed in her.

"That's quite a tale," Cody said when Makenzie finished.

"I know." Sharing the story with Cody, and feeling all the emotions that went with it, made Makenzie lightheaded. "I don't even want the ring anymore," she admitted.

Cody was quiet. Her hazel eyes studied Makenzie's face.

"Why don't you talk to Thomas instead of your mom?" Cody suggested, breaking the silence that filled the air between them.

"What?!" Makenzie's eyes grew wide. "Why would I do that?" She looked at Cody like she'd lost her mind.

"I know Thomas pretty well. From living here, I mean." Cody said quickly. "I'm sure he was shocked to learn you found the ring, especially when he saw you wearing it. But that was yesterday. I bet his anger has faded."

"But what if it hasn't?" Makenzie asked.

Cody hesitated, looking off in the distance, as if she'd find the answer there. She turned her gaze back to Makenzie.

"You could talk to him at the Baldwin Manor office. There would be other people around, so if he is still upset, he'd have to control his temper."

Makenzie rocked back and forth on the thin, rubber soles of her flip-flops, mulling over Cody's suggestion. There was a chance it could work. And she wouldn't have to call her parents.

"It might not be easy, but if you don't want the ring anymore, you could give it to him there," Cody said.

A smile bloomed on Makenzie's face. "You know, I think you might be right." She exhaled a sigh of relief, pleased the call was postponed. At least for now.

A smiling couple lingered nearby, reading the historic placard posted in front of the boathouse. Noticing their presence, Makenzie gave them a friendly nod.

"Better let you get to it. Thanks for listening and for the suggestion. You've been a huge help."

Cody beamed. "Good luck," she said, turning toward the couple.

Chapter Twenty-Three

Makenzie hurried toward Pinewood. Her feet on auto pilot, she jogged up the steps and through the cabin door while her thoughts swirled. *Am I crazy? Confronting Thomas after he got so angry when he saw the ring? How does it belong to him? At least he won't be expecting me,* Makenzie told herself, trying to build up her courage.

She reached into the front pouch of the backpack and retrieved the ring. Its stone twinkled, sky blue in the dim cabin light, almost like it was winking. Oddly, it gave her some much-needed encouragement. Makenzie studied the band. It was hard to believe her random find in the lake had led to this. With a sigh, she slipped it deep into the front pocket of her faded jean shorts.

Part gift shop, part museum and office, the wooden structure's heavy metal door was propped open, inviting visitors inside. Aged floorboards creaked when walked upon due to the weight of countless tourists who had strolled through the adjoining rooms over the years.

The first room housed a small selection of books about the Lake Tahoe area and historic manor. Postcards and trinkets, along with colourful clothing and hats, embellished with *Baldwin Manor ~ Celebrating 100 Years* were displayed on nearby shelves. Makenzie smiled at a poster advertising the upcoming Roaring 20s event featuring partygoers dressed in vintage clothing.

The second room was steeped in history, its walls a photo gallery of the Baldwin family from the early 1900s to the 1960s when the manor was bequeathed to the U.S. Forest Service to preserve and maintain. The black and white images, portals to a bygone era, captured its subjects for future generations to speculate what life was like back in the day.

The portrait of a handsome man in a top hat caught Makenzie's eye, the lapels on his sepia toned jacket wide across his broad chest. Intrigued, she paused to study his face, which somehow looked familiar. *James Baldwin, 1922 to 2003* the plaque under the frame read.

Quit stalling. You're almost there.

Makenzie took a deep breath and passed through the last door, entering a smaller room that functioned as the Baldwin Manor office. Colourful photos of the property's many buildings decorated the walls. A few folding chairs lined the wall near a small window on the left side of the room.

Thomas stood behind a wooden counter that split the space in two, his head bent, reading. Makenzie stopped at the sight of him. Her heart raced. *I can do this.* She scanned the room, taking in a small door to the right of the counter that led to the adjacent courtyard. The muffled voices of people milling around outside was comforting. Taking in a deep breath gave her the touch of bravery she needed to approach the counter.

The time-worn floor boards creaked under the weight of Makenzie's footsteps, alerting Thomas. He stopped reading and raised his head. A look of surprise flashed across his face, then turned to anger.

"What do you want?" he growled. He scanned her hands, appearing to search for the ring, which wasn't there.

Makenzie gulped, thankful for the counter that separated them. "T-t-o talk to you," she blurted. "About the ring."

"I don't have anything to say to you." His furious eyes drilled into Makenzie's for an instant. He looked down at the papers, dismissing her.

Determined to uncover the truth, Makenzie reached into her pocket and pulled out the ring. "I want to know how this is yours?" she said matter-of-factly, holding the band out in front of her. The stone, sky blue in her cabin minutes before, had changed to a deep sapphire.

The animosity emanating from Thomas deflated when he saw the ring. The edges of his hard eyes softened. Encouraged, Makenzie slowly stepped forward and set the band down on the stack of papers he was reading, then took a step back.

Thomas reached for the ring. His fingers, thick from years of manual labour, picked it up gently, as if it was made of glass. Mesmerized, Makenzie watched him examine the band with a look of wonder, like he was seeing it for the first time. His eyes glimmered with the beginnings of tears that didn't fall.

Stunned by his unexpected reaction, the courage Makenzie needed to confront him was replaced by curiosity. The pace of her heartbeat slowed from a nervous gallop to a gentle trot. A feeling of kindness washed over her and softened her toward him.

"Please," Makenzie said softly. "Tell me how the ring belongs to you."

Thomas looked up and focused his blurry eyes on Makenzie. "It was mine. Until I gave it to the love of my life."

Chapter Twenty-Four

akenzie gasped. Thomas' admission was a complete shock. An invisible cloud of silence filled the space between them while her mind reeled. *If he gave the ring to someone he loved, how did I find it in the lake?* Although the office was warm, goosebumps prickled the skin on her arms.

Taking in the distressed look in Thomas' eyes as he stared silently at the ring, Makenzie searched for what to say. She eyed the chairs in the corner of the office.

"Would you like to sit down?" she asked.

Thomas nodded. Still clutching the ring, he walked out from behind the counter and sat on one of the metal folding chairs. It groaned under his weight. Makenzie pulled a chair out from the wall and sat a few feet in front of him.

Thomas let out a slow breath, his eyes focused on the ring, and began.

"Throughout all the years I've searched, I never really thought I'd find it." A melancholy smile tugged at the corners of his mouth. "Holding it again takes me back in time, like it was just yesterday that I lost it, and her. Forever."

"Who did you lose?" Makenzie said softly, as if she was talking to a young child.

"Her name was Dakota," Thomas whispered, raising his head to look at her.

Dakota. The name sounded familiar. *Where have I heard it before?*

Makenzie squirmed in her chair. It was uncomfortable to meet his gaze. The sorrow in his eyes was a complete switch from the anger they held before.

"What happened to her?" she prodded gently.

Thomas sighed. He looked away as if searching for the answer before he turned back toward Makenzie.

"When I was 20, I was hired on to the crew tasked with building Camp Baldwin. Because it's located near the manor, members of the Baldwin family would visit periodically to see our progress. One of the spectators was Dakota, the granddaughter of William Baldwin, the family's patriarch who built Baldwin Manor."

Makenzie nodded, encouraging Thomas to continue.

"I was enamoured by her. I don't know what she saw in me, but Dakota would stop by the construction site around the time my work day ended. We'd sit on the sand by the lake and talk. Sometimes for hours. She was smart and witty. Really down to earth, although she came from a wealthy family. In the beginning, our differences bothered me. But the more I got to know her, I realized it didn't matter. To us. But it would have been a problem for her parents, especially her father. It wasn't just that I didn't have a college education, I didn't come from a prominent family either."

"That seems kind of old-fashioned," Makenzie said. "Her parent's way of thinking, I mean."

"Things were different back then. Her parents grew up in San Francisco's society scene. Spending time at the Baldwin Manor only in the summer months, when they'd invite their well-to-do friends to stay. All too soon, the camp was finished. Which meant I wouldn't be able to see Dakota as easily. That's where the ring comes in." Thomas looked down at the band. It looked small in his hand. He took in a deep breath and continued.

"I'd received a hefty final pay cheque when the camp was completed. Wanting to express my love, I spent most of the money on the ring. There were so many to choose from, but when the clerk at the jewelry store showed me this, I knew it was the one."

Makenzie looked at the band resting in Thomas' palm. The stone, a dark sapphire hue when she'd set it on the counter minutes before, was less vivid. A lighter shade of blue.

"The heart-shaped stone is an alexandrite, rare, like Dakota,"

Thomas said. "It also reminded me of where we met, because it changes colour, like the lake as the water gets deeper."

Because she already knew the stone was made of a mineral that enabled it to morph into different colours, Makenzie simply nodded. Entranced by his story, she was afraid if she spoke, she'd break the spell of his tale.

"When we'd meet, we stayed near the manor or camp, but I wanted that night to be special, so we went out on the lake in a paddle boat, a full moon lighting our way. I gave Dakota the ring and promised I'd find a way for us to be together, somehow. She was delighted. With the gift, and with me."

Thomas' shoulders slumped. He raked the fingers of his free hand through his short white hair. "I didn't know the happiest moment of my life would be followed by the worst."

He turned his head in the direction of the lake, eyes bright under a veil of tears that didn't fall.

"It was late when we returned. I watched Dakota walk down the boat dock and up the stairs to the manor, the full moon illuminating her way. She turned at the top of the stairs and gave me a wave. Then the front door opened, and her father walked out."

Makenzie's gaze, focused on the ring, lifted to look at Thomas. A feeling of déjà vu washed over her. His story was familiar.

"I remember it like it was yesterday. In few quick strides, he reached Dakota, who he'd caught returning home by surprise. He grabbed her waving arm in mid-air, swung her around to face him, then grasped her by the elbows, rooting her in place. The ring, positioned between them, was visible in the moonlight, giving away our secret. For a moment, time stood still. Then he held her wrist with one hand and yanked the ring off her finger with the other. Dakota wrestled away from his grasp, turned, and ran down the stairs toward the dock."

Makenzie's brow furrowed. *Why do I know this?* She struggled to remember and pay attention at the same time

"I started to run toward her, but was tugged backwards by the rope I held in my hand. It was tied to the bow of the paddle boat. I'd untied it from the dock moments before to return to Camp Baldwin so no one would find us out. It only took a couple of seconds to reknot the line, but by then it was too late."

"What do you mean, too late?" Makenzie asked. But she already knew.

"I turned and saw it happen," Thomas said, his voice almost a whisper.

"Dakota was looking down the dock at me, not at where she was going. She didn't see the tangle of rope until her foot got caught in it. I watched her jerk to a stop, but the momentum of her running pulled her upper body forward, and she toppled. Hitting her head on one of the metal cleats that juts out of the dock with a horrible thud." Thomas winced. His shoulders shook as the tears that threatened to fall earlier trickled silently down his weathered cheeks.

It's my dream. A sudden chill gripped Makenzie's heart, making her shudder. *That's why his story is so familiar.*

"I'm so sorry, Thomas," Makenzie said softly. "Dakota died, didn't she?"

Thomas nodded his head slowly.

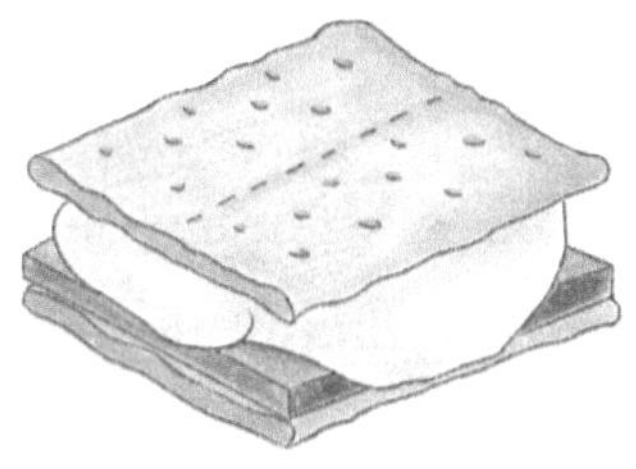

Chapter Twenty-Five

Makenzie stared at the ring resting in the palm of Thomas' upturned hand. The threads of her history with it entwined together like the strands of a rope. The afternoon she'd found it and her overwhelming compulsion to keep it, although hidden. Her dreams about a vintage girl named Dakota that came to her after she'd slipped on the band before falling asleep. The stone changing colour. It all made sense.

"I saw Dakota fall," Makenzie said, looking up at him. "In a dream. A nightmare really. Somehow, I think the ring was showing me its past."

With a pained expression on his face, Thomas' eyes gazed past Makenzie, as if he was reliving the dreadful scene.

"I ran toward her," he continued, "but her father was there in an instant. He stood over her, yelling at me to leave, and he threw the ring. It soared over my head, landing in the lake. I didn't learn she was gone until a few days later. The life I'd hoped we'd build together perished along with her." Thomas looked down at the band, emotionally spent.

Makenzie's heart felt heavy with the weight of Thomas' tragedy. The ring, a beautiful random find in the lake, was the keeper of a dark secret, now revealed.

"What did you do then?" Makenzie asked softly, hoping to nudge him out of the depths of his sorrow.

His damp eyes raised to meet hers. "Although Dakota was gone, I couldn't leave. There was a housing boom, so I threw myself into it to forget her. In theory, it was a good plan. But during the countless hours I spent building hundreds of structures, my thoughts were about her and the life we could have had." Thomas sighed.

"After the devastating accident, the Baldwin family stopped visiting Lake Tahoe. Ultimately, they donated the manor to the U.S. Forest Service to be preserved as a historic landmark for future generations. Because of my experience building the camp, I was hired to oversee the property until it transitioned to the Forest Service. After that, I stayed on, employed at the manor in various roles, enabling me to search for the ring in my spare time. I never thought I'd find it. And then, there it was, on your finger." His eyes locked on Makenzie's face. "I'm truly sorry I scared you yesterday. It was quite a shock to see it after all these years." He plucked the band from his palm with his free hand, reached over, and gently placed it on Makenzie's knee.

She looked down. The stone had changed to an iridescent ice blue, a shade Makenzie hadn't seen before. It was as if Thomas' story had cleared the ring of its wretched history. His tale left her numb, full of questions she didn't know if she should ask. Timidly, she picked up the ring.

"Thomas," Makenzie paused, searching for the right words, then continued. "Did you hate Dakota's father for what he did?"

"Yes, at first. But he was protecting his daughter. He didn't know me, or how much I loved Dakota, or how happy we were together. I blamed myself. If we hadn't gone out in the boat, if I hadn't given her the ring, she would still be with me."

Makenzie picked up the band she was never meant to keep.

"I know this won't bring Dakota back," Makenzie said, extending her closed fist toward Thomas. "But I hope it gives you some peace." She unclenched her fingers over his upturned palm, and placed the ring in his hand.

Thomas' eyes widened in surprise, then softened, glowing with gratitude. He looked at Makenzie and smiled. The one she'd challenged herself to get the day they'd met.

Chapter Twenty-Six

Walking slowly along the dusty path to camp, Makenzie couldn't stop thinking about Thomas' tragic story. How frightening to watch the love of your life trip and fall, and not find out until days later she had died.

She couldn't imagine the anguish he must have gone through. The life Thomas had dreamed of, gone in an instant. Like a bright flame atop a newly lit candlestick, extinguished too soon. And then to live with it your entire life. Makenzie shuddered. Now she understood why he was so lonely.

While her thoughts were consumed with Thomas and the life he'd lost, she couldn't help thinking about Dakota's father. Even though he was only trying to protect his daughter, his actions triggered her accidental death. Of course the family never returned to the Baldwin Manor. Why would they want to be reminded of Dakota's tragic fate every time they looked at the boat dock? The serene setting had been poisoned by painful memories.

The emotional events of the morning behind her, Makenzie remembered it was Saturday. Her parents were expecting her to call. She was late; it was almost noon. Off the hook now that she'd given the ring to Thomas, she was relieved they'd never need to know she'd found the band and uncovered its unimaginable history.

Makenzie turned around. Picking up her pace, she headed in the direction of the boat dock. The thick growth of pine trees thinned out along the path as she got closer.

Her heart felt lighter than it had in weeks. The angst from earlier in the morning when she'd planned to call home had vanished, along with the mental burden of hiding the ring and worrying if she'd be able to keep it. It hadn't occurred to her until then how finding the band had changed her over the summer. She smiled, content with herself and the outcome she had been so stressed out about. Thomas had the ring and she finally had his smile.

Rounding the path that led to the dock, Makenzie saw Cody standing in front of the boathouse gazing at the turquoise water. Even though she was late, Makenzie jogged over.

When Cody turned towards her, Makenzie was surprised by her friend's troubled expression. "Hi. Did I catch you at a bad time?"

"Oh, hello. I've been thinking about you. How did it go with

Thomas?" Cody's brow was furrowed with concern. "Was he still angry?"

"Nope. It was really interesting. But complicated."

Makenzie's phone, tucked in the back pocket of her shorts, began to ring. She swiped it out and read the display. *Dad*. She clicked the side button, sending him to voicemail.

"Ugh, I'm late checking in. I'll come back later when we can talk. But please don't worry, everything is okay."

Cody's face brightened, erasing the crease between her brows. She nodded at Makenzie with a smile.

Makenzie hurried up the few worn steps to the dock. A chill snaked along her back when she neared the weathered metal cleat that protruded skyward from the edge of the wooden structure. Knowing what had happened there, even though it was decades ago, was unsettling. She was thankful her visits to the spot were ending. With just a week of camp remaining, she'd only need to check in with her parents one more time.

Seated on the edge of the dock, legs dangling over the side above the water, Makenzie looked at the façade of the Baldwin Manor in the distance. Still grappling with Thomas' tale, she couldn't stop thinking about how heartbroken Dakota's father must have been, knowing he caused his daughter's death. All because he was trying to protect her from what he thought would bring her harm.

She tapped a few buttons on the front screen of her phone and listened to it ring.

"Hey, kiddo. I just left a message. Thought I'd hear from you by now. How's it going?" On speaker mode, her father's words floated into the air, taking Makenzie by surprise. They wrapped around her like an invisible hug, warm and comforting after discovering the dreadful reality of Thomas and his lost love.

"Hi, Dad. Things are great. Sorry I didn't pick up before."

"Just one more week at camp. You behaving yourself?"

The frustration she usually felt when being questioned was replaced by something new. Understanding. Her parents just wanted to protect her. Keep her safe. Checking up on her was the only way they knew how.

Makenzie smiled. "Of course. Although I do need to get some swim practice in today. I've had a busy morning."

"That's my girl. Keep up the good work. Your mom and I are really looking forward to your coming home. We've missed you."

Instead of feeling looked down upon, Makenzie basked in the praise of her father's words. "Me too, Dad." Her heart soared.

"Isn't there a big event coming up?"

"The Baldwin Manor 100th Anniversary Celebration to be exact. Festivities start next week. It's going to be awesome. I'm helping out at the Roaring 20s dance party. How's Mom?"

A wave of homesickness washed over Makenzie as she listened to her father with restored affection. She really was looking forward to seeing her parents and to going home.

After the call, Makenzie lingered at the dock. She looked down at her hands absentmindedly. Not wearing the ring would take some getting used to. She thought back to the day she'd found it, mesmerized by its beauty and her overwhelming desire to keep it—enough to lie to Hannah about turning the band in—followed by the series of odd dreams. It all made sense. The dreams started when she fell asleep wearing the band. Somehow, it revealed its dark past to her subconscious.

Makenzie smiled. *I was meant to find the ring so I could return it to its rightful owner, Thomas.*

Chapter Twenty-Seven

Makenzie surveyed the calm, mirror-like surface of Lake Tahoe. At her feet, its sea glass hues came together, creating a rainbow of blue. Translucent under the dock where she stood, the water morphed into a blue-green turquoise shade before turning a deep indigo farther out. She took in a deep breath and dove, bracing herself for the numbing chill that caused her skin to break out in head-to-toe goosebumps.

Swimming out to the orange buoy that bobbed in the distance, then back to Camp Baldwin's boat dock, Makenzie's thoughts meandered from the upcoming anniversary celebration to Hannah. The last week of camp would be much more fun if she hadn't ruined their friendship by lying about the ring and hiding it. But she didn't regret reuniting Thomas with the band after learning its tragic history. She had merely played a small role in its sad biography.

The metal clang of the Chuck House triangle sounded in the distance, interrupting her practice. Makenzie dried off and hurried to Pinewood to change, arriving at the Chuck House just in time to grab a grilled ham and cheese, bag of chips, and fruit before the lunch service ended. Most of the other counsellors had already finished eating by the time she scanned the dining room for a place to sit.

A few tables over, Hannah and Naomi sat together chatting. *It's now or never.* Makenzie took in a deep breath and walked over.

"Hey you two, how's it going?" Makenzie asked. She scanned Naomi's face, then Hannah's. By the looks of her plate, she'd been late getting to the Chuck House too.

"Hey, Kenzie," Naomi said. "We were just talking about how the summer flew by. Hard to believe it's our last week."

"I know, crazy huh? Mind if I sit here?" Makenzie asked, searching Hannah's face for a reaction.

"Of course not," Naomi said. "I'm meeting up with Grace in a few at Cabin Row." She stood, sliding her tray off the side of the table. "See you at check in."

Hannah looked down at her half-eaten sandwich, avoiding Makenzie's gaze. "I know you're still upset I lied to you," Makenzie began awkwardly.

Hannah lifted her head. Speechless, she gave Makenzie a blank stare. Her silence was unnerving. Makenzie had nothing to lose. Hannah would either understand why she'd felt compelled to keep the ring, or she wouldn't. At least she had a chance to explain.

"At first, because the ring was so unusual, I really wanted it for myself. Sometimes, I'd wear it at night and the stone would change into different shades of blue-green. Then I started having those strange dreams I told you about when your mom found it. Do you remember? They were about a girl dressed in historic clothing. I didn't realize it at the time, but the dreams happened when I fell asleep wearing the band."

As she spoke, Makenzie searched Hannah's face for a reaction. Her previous flat stare, replaced by a flicker of interest, was encouraging.

"My last dream was a nightmare where the girl was running down the Baldwin Manor boat dock. She tripped and fell, hitting her head with a horrible thud on one of those metal cleats you tie a boat up to. I woke up shaking, not knowing how the dream ended."

"But it was just a dream," Hannah said, finally breaking her silence.

"That's what I thought. Until Thomas saw the ring on my finger and tried to take it from me."

Hannah frowned. "I don't understand. You turned it in to Mrs. White." Her narrowed eyes drilled into Makenzie.

"Nobody claimed it, so she gave me the ring on Friday afternoon, after you went home. Then, when I was helping Thomas string lights for the Roaring 20s party, he saw it and became angry. I was really scared," Makenzie confided.

"But he's always so quiet. That seems unlike him." Sensing Makenzie's discomfort, Hannah's green eyes softened.

"I know, that's what I thought. Because I couldn't talk to you about it, I decided to call my mom and tell her the whole story."

"Why didn't you tell Mrs. White?" Hannah asked.

"At some point, she'd call my parents about the ring I'd failed to turn in and they'd be disappointed in me. So I thought it would be better if I told them. But in the end, I didn't have to."

"I'm not following you," Hannah said.

"I ran into my friend Cody on the way to call my dad."

"Who's Cody?"

"You know, the girl who volunteers at the Baldwin Manor boathouse. She wears an old-fashioned, sailor-style dress and gives historic flyers to tourists?"

"Hmm, I've never seen her," Hannah said.

"I met her earlier this summer. She's usually at the boathouse on Saturdays when I swim and check in with my parents."

Hannah shook her head. "No clue. What does she have to do with Thomas?"

"I told her the story about the ring and how he tried to grab it from me. Because Cody knows Thomas from her time volunteering, she suggested I confront him about it instead of telling my parents."

"And?" Hannah asked, leaning over her untouched lunch tray, food forgotten.

"I did." Makenzie recounted their conversation in Thomas' office, ending with her giving him the ring.

Hannah was transfixed. "What a horrible story," she said, wincing. "You just never know what people experience in their past."

"Right? Imagine searching for something almost your whole life, and the shock of seeing it unexpectedly on someone's finger," Makenzie said.

Telling Hannah felt good. Like an invisible weight she didn't know she'd been carrying lifted with each word she spoke.

"You'll probably think I'm crazy, but I truly believe I was meant to find the ring so I could return it to Thomas," Makenzie said. A rosy bloom spread across her tanned cheeks as she searched Hannah's face for a reaction.

Hannah was silent. Even though she might still be mad, Makenzie realized it didn't matter. Ultimately, she'd done the right thing. Not turning the ring in when she first found it helped her get there. She picked up half of the now soggy grilled ham and cheese and took a bite.

"I don't think you're crazy," Hannah said, her eyes meeting Makenzie's. "A little weird maybe, but not crazy." A slow smile spread across her face. "Forgive me for being so rule oriented? I guess I kinda took the mentor thing a bit too far."

"Of course," Makenzie said with a grin. It was the best sandwich she'd ever tasted.

Chapter Twenty-Eight

"**I** can't believe camp ends tomorrow," Hannah said. Her eyes connected with Makenzie's in the reflection of the bathhouse mirror.

"I know. The summer went by way too fast," Makenzie said, returning the cap of the ruby red lipstick she'd just applied with a click. She turned to face Hannah. "How do I look?"

The crushed pink velvet of Makenzie's sleeveless, antique, drop-waisted dress trimmed in gold lace was striking against her sun-tanned skin. Ivory satin opera gloves extended up her bare arms, ending above her elbows. A hot pink, feathered boa draped around her neck completed her vintage look.

"Smashing, darling. Simply smashing," Hannah quipped with a mischievous grin.

At a meeting to review the 100th Anniversary Celebration, the woman in charge handed out a schedule of events, including a list of popular sayings from the era, which she encouraged volunteers to use throughout the evening.

"And you," Makenzie said taking a step back to take in Hannah's black beaded flapper girl costume, resplendent with a jewel-toned peacock feather affixed to the side of a headband that ran across her forehead. "You look like the bee's knees," she said with a smile, remembering the term from the handout. Back in the day it meant someone or something was marvellous.

"Thanks," Hannah said. "I'm lucky my mom kept this after a Halloween party she and my dad went to a few years ago." She shook her hips, sending the long fringe that accentuated the bottom of the short dress into a swaying motion. The over-sized strand of pearls she wore around her neck was a stark contrast against the shimmering black beads that decorated the front of the dress.

"Although, I don't think they wore tennis shoes back then," Makenzie said, looking down at her friend's black, low-top Chuck Taylors.

"Yeah, well, my mom wasn't about to buy matching dress shoes for one night."

"Same," Makenzie said. She reached over and picked her phone up off the shelf above the row of sinks. "Let's get a picture." The girls crowded together, ear to ear. Makenzie held the phone out, positioning their smiling faces on the reversed screen and took a snap. Checking the image, she noticed the time embedded at the top of the rectangle. "Ugh. It's 5:43, we're late!"

"Hopefully Naomi was on time," Hannah said, grabbing her backpack off the floor.

A blur of black and pink moved through the tree-lined path to the Baldwin Manor garden as the girls raced to the Roaring 20s party. Rushing past the boathouse, Makenzie saw Cody at her usual post, talking to Thomas. She waved a gloved hand, but they were deep in conversation and didn't notice her.

Makenzie hesitated. She wanted to stop, but music of the era floated through the air, reminding her she was late. *I'll catch up with Cody later so I can tell her about giving Thomas the ring.*

"Where have you been?" Naomi said. The smile pasted on her lips masked the growled question delivered through gritted teeth. "You're late."

"We were getting dressed and lost track of time," Makenzie whispered, taking a seat next to her at the check-in table.

"I can help whoever's next," Makenzie said, looking down the growing line of costumed guests who stood waiting in front of the table. A tall gentleman in a black top hat and tuxedo side-stepped over from Naomi's line and stood in front of Makenzie.

"Good evening, sir," Makenzie said, giving him an apologetic smile. "Sorry for the wait. Your name, please."

Next to her, Hannah slid into the empty chair and beckoned to the next person in line. The check-in process flowed smoothly with the three of them working together. Makenzie let out a sigh of relief when the last guest was marked off the list. She swivelled in the chair to watch the dance party, now in full swing. On either side of her, Hannah and Naomi turned to take in the spectacle.

Revellers from the bygone era whirled, arm in arm, across a black and white parquet dance floor, dancing the foxtrot. The checkered flooring, laid out in the middle of the manor's immense lawn, was accentuated by round tables draped in shimmery gold cloths where guests lingered, sipping on lemon-coloured cocktails.

A DJ, white shirt sleeves rolled up under thick pinstriped suspenders, sporting a black fedora, spun music of the times from a raised platform near the stage. The light strings Makenzie and Naomi helped Thomas hang in the canopy of pines dangled overhead, adding a festive glow to the celebration.

"How do they know those dance moves?" Makenzie asked, eyes glued to the costumed pairs that glided effortlessly around the dance floor.

"I have no clue," Naomi answered. "Looks kinda complicated to me."

"Most of the attendees are die-hard 1920s fans. They know all the dances of the time," Mrs. White said.

The girls turned to find the camp director standing in front of the table. Makenzie gulped down a sudden urge to laugh, covering her mouth with a gloved hand.

Mrs. White's usual camo camp shirt, khaki pants, and boots

were replaced by a deep burgundy satin dress that flowed past her knees. The style of the gown was made to drape off a taller, more slender figure. A large, shiny gold bow hung from the curve of her hip, its fabric stopping just above black, patent leather, T-strap pumps, which appeared to be a half-size too small. A gold velvet shawl covered her sturdy shoulders, complimenting the bow. Red rhinestone and diamond drop earrings dangled from her ears, and a matching necklace hung from her neck.

"I know," Mrs. White said with a sigh, in response to Makenzie's reaction. She tugged at the snug non-bow side of the dress. "I drag this get-up out periodically for these events. Seems like it gets tighter each time." She studied the girls in their finery. "Don't you three look lovely. Have all the guests checked in?"

"Yep, and I think you look fabulous, Mrs. W," Hannah said, giving her a wink.

"You're too kind. Thanks for all your help. You can stay and enjoy the festivities or head back for the last campfire of the summer. There'll be s'mores."

Relieved of their volunteer duties, the girls lingered at the periphery of the makeshift checkered floor, watching a few of the outdated dances.

"Imagine being excited to do that." Makenzie pointed at a woman standing with her legs apart, bent at the knees, crisscrossing her hands to either knee when they came together.

"Looks kinda like the chicken dance, but with knees," Hannah said.

"It's called the Charleston," Naomi answered. "I watched my grandma do those moves at my cousin's wedding with my uncle. They're into all that old timey stuff. I don't know about you two, but I'm ready for a s'more."

"Sounds good," Makenzie said. "Come on, Hannah, let's go."

"According to that list of 1920s terms, this is what's called a '23 Skidoo,'" Hannah said, opening her backpack. She fished out her flashlight, then turned toward camp, leading the trio back on the path that flanked the lake.

Makenzie searched for Cody as they passed the boathouse, but she wasn't there. It was late, so she must have left. *Hopefully I'll catch her in the morning before my parents arrive to take me home.* Her parents. A smile spread across her face. Instead of feeling annoyed by their overprotectiveness, she was looking forward to seeing them. But at that moment, what she was really looking forward to was biting into a gooey s'more.

Chapter Twenty-Nine

The metallic clanging of the Chuck House triangle woke Makenzie out of a deep sleep. She burrowed into the warmth of her sleeping bag, not wanting to let go of the fuzzy images from the early morning dream that lingered in her waking consciousness.

Dressed in their 1920s finery, she and Hannah were on a black-and-white checkered dance floor, performing one of the dances of the era. Oddly, Cody was there too, in her navy sailor dress.

Last night's party must have seeped into my subconscious while I slept.

Her disappointment in not being able to talk with Cody about what happened when she confronted Thomas about the ring must have invited her into the dream.

Makenzie threw on her Camp Baldwin sweatshirt and pulled

her sweatpants on to fend off the crisp morning air. It was hard to believe she'd be sleeping in her own bed later that night. She couldn't decide if the empty feeling in her core was due to her hollow stomach or the anticipation of going home.

Hannah was already halfway through breakfast when Makenzie plopped her tray of food on the table across from her.

"You're up early," Makenzie said. She grabbed a slice of raisin toast off her plate and bit into it to appease her growling belly.

"My mom's picking me up soon. I'm helping her out at a jewelry show this afternoon."

"Sounds fun. I'll be on a plane back to Arizona." Makenzie scooped a mound of scrambled eggs onto her fork. "I'm sure going to miss waking up to a home-cooked breakfast every day, and you too." She gave Hannah a quick smile before devouring the bite of eggs.

Hannah put her hand over her heart and pretended to look hurt. "Nice to know you'll miss the food more than me."

"Nah, I'll miss you more. Are you coming back next summer?"

"For sure. What about you?" Hannah asked, draining the juice from her cup.

"I really hope so. Maybe Jessica will come too. That is, if she ever talks to me again." Makenzie sighed. She hadn't forgotten Jess was mad at her. She'd just tucked it away, since she couldn't do anything about it while she was at camp.

"I gotta go." Hannah stood. "I'm really bad at goodbyes. How about, I'll see you next year?"

Makenzie nodded her head. "See you next year."

She jumped off the bench and wrapped her arms around Hannah in a quick hug. Returning to her half-eaten breakfast, she glimpsed the large, round, classroom-style clock that hung above the barn door of the Chuck House. If she was going to say goodbye to Cody and Thomas before her parents arrived, she'd need to hurry.

On her way to the boathouse, Makenzie gazed at the lake's indigo surface. Free of boats and swimmers in the early morning, it looked like glass. She breathed in the fresh scent of pine, and took a mental snapshot to remember when she was home.

Only the vintage brass padlock securing the door to the boathouse greeted her when the structure came into view. Makenzie's heart sank. *Maybe I'll catch Cody on my way back to camp.*

Continuing toward the Baldwin Manor in search of Thomas, she walked up the path to his cottage and knocked. Her eyes scanned the surrounding area while she waited for the door to swing open. No answer. She knocked again, harder this time.

"Hello, Thomas. Are you home?" The cawing of a crow flying overhead was the only response.

Hoping he might be in the adjacent shed, Makenzie wandered around to the side door. It was ajar, inviting her in.

"Hello? Thomas?" she said, stepping into the dimly lit space.

Makenzie crinkled her nose at the musty smell that emanated from the hard-packed dirt floor. Worn wooden shelves, stocked with tools and bins of nails and screws lined the back wall. Walking further into the space, her fingertips brushed the dusty seat of an antiquated riding mower parked in the middle of the structure, waiting to be ridden out of the side barn door. An assortment of shovels, rakes, and a garden hoe leaned together in a corner conspiratorially. A faint beam of light filtering in from a small skylight illuminated the dust particles that swirled around Makenzie's feet when she stopped. He wasn't there.

As she turned to leave, her gaze fell on a small shelf, tucked in the corner by the door. A framed oval photograph, out of place among the tools and equipment, rested at eye level. Intrigued, she reached out and grasped the sepia portrait, bringing it closer to inspect the image.

Makenzie gasped. She closed her eyes tight, then opened them again, making sure she wasn't imagining things. Her heart raced. She walked a few steps toward the open door, tilting the frame in the daylight to get a better look, fingers tingling around the black oval.

Cody stood in front of the boathouse, grinning, next to a man dressed in work clothes. His smile mirrored hers. It was a face she recognized, only much younger.

"Makenzie," Thomas said quietly.

She jumped, grasping the antique frame as it almost toppled out of her hand. Riveted by the unbelievable image, she hadn't noticed

Thomas standing outside the doorway. Her eyes narrowed, studying the outline of his face, then returned to the photograph. It trembled in her shaking hands.

"How is this even possible?" Her voice shook as she shoved the frame in his direction. "Cody is Dakota. But how?"

"I don't know," Thomas said. His eyes soft and apologetic. "I discovered her years ago, when I started working at the manor, after the family moved. Somehow, she appears at the boathouse every summer around the time I gave her the ring."

Makenzie's confused eyes searched the photograph while Thomas spoke. There was no denying his words. She knew Cody. Dakota. The same girl she'd befriended over the summer smiled back at her from the black and white image taken decades before.

"She was searching for the ring the day I found her. As crazy as it sounds, I believe Dakota is suspended in time, the ring binding her to her past life," Thomas said gently.

Makenzie flashed on the night before when she saw them, deep in conversation at the boathouse. Her attempt to get their attention had been unsuccessful. Now she knew why.

She tilted her head, meeting Thomas' gaze. "I stopped by the boathouse on my way here, to say goodbye. It was Cody," Makenzie gulped, "I mean Dakota, who suggested I talk to you about the ring. She wasn't there."

A heaviness crept into Makenzie's heart. The confusion she'd felt moments before was replaced by numbing sadness.

"I gave the ring to her last night. I don't know how, but it's why Dakota stayed. I don't think she'll be back."

Makenzie stared at Thomas, letting his words sit in the place where the unbelievable is believable. Her eyes burned with the sting of tears. Cody, her friend, was gone.

"You've lost her again," Makenzie said, wiping her wet cheeks with the back of her hand.

"Yes, but it's different this time. She'll always be in my heart."

Unprepared for Makenzie's tears, Thomas fished a handkerchief from his pocket and handed it to her. "You've lost her too. I wasn't aware you'd become friends."

Makenzie sniffled, wiping away the remainder of her tears. She handed the white square of fabric back to Thomas.

"I didn't know her that well, but it's shocking that the girl in your story, Dakota, was Cody. And to think her dad was responsible for the accident." Makenzie's heart ached.

"I know Dakota's father never imagined his anger would do her harm. It was all so unfortunate. If only we'd talked to him about our relationship instead of keeping it a secret. Things could have ended differently." Thomas gave Makenzie a hopeful smile. "Please don't be sad. She wouldn't want that. You helped return the ring and Dakota's where she needs to be, at peace.

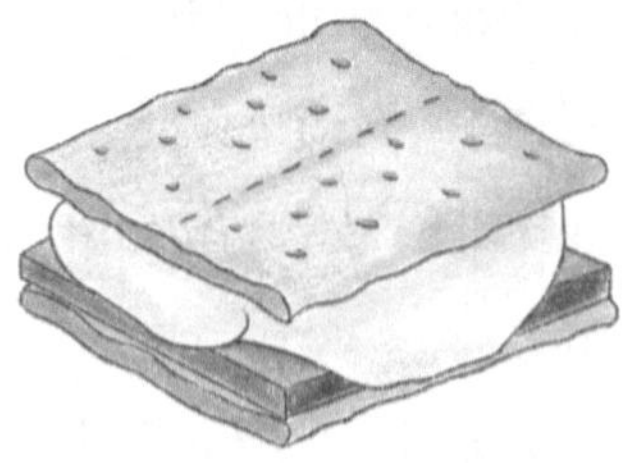

Chapter Thirty

Makenzie haphazardly shoved her clothes into the camo duffle bag, while the morning's events swirled in her mind like the colours on a lollipop. She knew the last day of camp would be tough, but nothing had prepared her for today.

Saying goodbye to Hannah at breakfast had been bittersweet, but she couldn't stop thinking about Thomas' startling revelation.

Imagine your whole life being altered in the blink of an eye, then discovering the person you thought you'd lost had never really left, but couldn't be with you the way you envisioned. Admiration for Thomas swelled in Makenzie's chest. He didn't want the ring for himself, he wanted to return it to Dakota. To release his love from the enchanted half-life that kept her suspended in time, even though it meant he'd never see her again. And she wouldn't see him again either.

Dakota and Cody being one and the same was the final piece of the surreal puzzle. Cody always wearing the same dress. Perpetually hanging out near the boathouse. Hannah not knowing who she was. The night she'd glimpsed a glowing figure on the beach. It all made sense now.

Lost in the tangled web of her thoughts, Makenzie didn't hear the wooden stairs leading up to Pinewood's small porch creak under the weight of her parents' footsteps. Her father tapped on the screen door to get her attention. Makenzie looked up, startled by their grinning faces peering at her through the screen's grey mesh.

"Ready to go home?" her father asked.

Happiness swelled in Makenzie's chest at the sight of her parents. A wide smile bloomed across her face. She flung open the screen door and flew into her father's outstretched arms.

"It's so good to see you," Makenzie said, untangling herself from her dad's embrace so she could give her mom a hug. And it really was. Their overprotectiveness was their way of showing her their love. She understood that now. Dakota's heartbreaking story was proof. She could never tell them, she realized; they'd never believe it.

"So, this is where you spent the summer," her mom said, surveying the cabin after Makenzie gave her one last squeeze and let her go. Blue eyes that mirrored her daughter's scanned the small space, stopping on a large banner that hung over Makenzie's bed. Multi-coloured sentiments written by Pinewood campers were splashed across the thick paper. Lovingly wrinkled from weeks of attention, it was affixed to the wall by a swath of masking tape at each corner. She read a few of the messages surrounded by doodles and smiley faces.

Thanks for all the fun! ~Emerson
I'll miss you, Kenzie. ~Charlotte
C U next year! ~Mikayla

"From the looks of it, I'd say you and your cabinmates had a great summer," her mom said, taking in each handwritten message.

"We did," Makenzie said wistfully, studying the banner. She glanced at Mikayla's message. "Hopefully you'll let me come back next year." She looked quickly from parent to parent, studying their reaction.

Her father chuckled. "We'll see, Kenzie," he said with a smile. His usual overprotective comments about her behaving and staying safe didn't follow. Maybe the summer spent apart had changed her parents too.

"What about me?" Jessica said. "Can I come too?" She opened the screen door, entering Pinewood with a sheepish grin.

"Jess!"

Makenzie nearly tackled her with an enormous bear hug, which was returned just as enthusiastically.

"What are you doing here?" she asked, pulling away so she

could look down at Jessica's feet. Her friend's signature style of wearing basketball shoes year-round applied even in August. "Your leg, it's healed."

"Yeah. The cast finally came off. Lots of physical therapy now and I'll be as good as new." Jessica looked around the cabin, stopping at the banner. She tilted her head to read a message one of the campers had scrawled up the side.

"You're the best!" Jessica read out loud. "Ella sure got that right."

She turned to face Makenzie. "I'm sorry I got so mad. It wasn't you that made me angry. I was upset because I missed spending the summer with you. And all of that." Jessica waved her hand toward the banner. "Forgive me?" she said sheepishly.

"Always!" Makenzie couldn't stop smiling. "You still haven't said why you're here. It's awesome. But why?"

"We wanted to surprise you," Makenzie's mom said. She looked at Jessica and nodded.

"Well," Jessica began. "Our parents met and they thought it would be a good idea if I visited where I'd be spending next summer. Actually, where we'd be spending next summer."

"No way, really?" Makenzie took in the three excited faces that stared back at her.

"Really," they said in unison.

Makenzie tossed her backpack in the car. Knowing she'd be back with Jess the following summer was almost overwhelming. She couldn't be happier. The grin that permeated her face was proof.

"All set?" her dad asked, approaching the car while her mother and Jessica trailed behind.

"Yep. And Dad, thanks for a great summer." Makenzie looked across the hood of the car at her father with a heartfelt smile.

"You're welcome," he said, returning his daughter's grin.

The car slowly wound up the camp's long drive. Its passengers settled in a comfortable silence; lost in their own thoughts.

"I almost forgot." Jessica looked down at Makenzie's bare hands. "Where's that ring you found?"

Makenzie's stomach tightened. She looked out the car window at the lake's indigo surface, shimmering in the afternoon sun. The keeper of a ghostly secret for decades, until she'd found the ring, ending its haunting legacy.

Makenzie turned. Her eyes focused on Jessica's questioning gaze.

"Oh, have I got a story to tell you," she whispered.

Acknowledgements

Thank you reader for heading to Camp Baldwin with Makenzie to experience her summer of mystery, friendship, and self-discovery.

I am forever grateful to my amazing publisher, Alanna Rusnak of Chicken House Press, for believing in my story and bringing *Makenzie's Ring* into the world. A dream come true, thank you! Alanna was supportive of every request, and championed my vision for the book. I couldn't have asked for a more inspirational and collaborative publishing partnership.

A huge shout out to Thais Derich, for starting our accountability group just before the pandemic, and to Marianne Lonsdale and Meghen Kurtzig for your continued presence weekdays on Zoom. Our early morning check-ins, followed by writing time, got my butt in the chair and were essential to finishing, revising, and querying the book. Your insightful encouragement and friendship over the years has been, and continues to be, invaluable.

Much appreciation to the dynamic writing community that was the Write on Mamas. From educational events, to hundreds of hours spent in-person at writing meet-ups, the group's supportive environment positively influenced my publication journey.

Special thanks to *Makenzie's Ring* beta readers; Nicole Baxter, Alex deLeuze, Rina Faletti, Stephanie Getzler, Kiley and Fiona Heliotes, Meghen Kurtzig, Jennifer Maruno, Amber Lea Starfire, and Jeanne Stevens, whose thoughtful critiques and suggestions helped shape the story along the way.

Tremendous thanks to Evy Warshawski for the insightful book launch pre-publicity. My heartfelt gratitude to Hilary Homzie, whose support of the book during its developmental and final stages has been invaluable. And to Jen Malone, much appreciation for being an inspirational mentor during the Big Sur Children's Writing Workshop.

Heartfelt props to Mikayla Stevens for her artistic talent on the whimsical chapter break illustrations and Camp Baldwin map. Thanks for bringing your creativity to the book!

To my mom, thank you for taking Cindy and me to the library when we were very young, which instilled a lifelong love of reading at an early age. And to my dad, who gave me my first dictionary.

Last, but definitely not least, infinite thanks to my wonderful husband Bill, son Alex, and daughters Emerson and Mikayla, for their encouragement, unending support and mutual love of a well-crafted s'more!

About the Author

Teri Stevens devoured s'mores and creepy stories as a child during summer camp at Lake Tahoe, CA. *Makenzie's Ring*, a ghostly story of friendship and self-discovery, is her debut novel. When she's not writing or exploring haunted manors, she's caring for her three teenagers, husband, backyard chickens and Maxx, their rescue dog. Visit her in Napa Valley, CA or at teristevens.co.

www.ingramcontent.com/pod-product-compliance
Lightning Source LLC
Chambersburg PA
CBHW020803310726
48969CB00002B/683